THE BORROWERS AFLOAT

THE
BORROWERS AFLOAT

Mary Norton

ILLUSTRATED BY BETH AND JOE KRUSH

AN ODYSSEY/HARCOURT BRACE YOUNG CLASSIC

HARCOURT BRACE & COMPANY

SAN DIEGO   NEW YORK   LONDON

First Harcourt Brace Young Classics edition 1998
First Odyssey Classics edition 1990
First published 1959

Library of Congress Cataloging-in-Publication Data
Norton, Mary.
The Borrowers afloat/Mary Norton; illustrated by Beth and Joe Krush.
p. cm.
"An Odyssey/Harcourt Brace Young Classic."
Sequel to "The Borrowers afield."
Summary: The Borrowers, a family of miniature people, journey down
a drain, live briefly in a teakettle, and are swept away in a flood
before finding a new home.
ISBN 0-15-210345-7   ISBN 0-15-210534-4 (pb)
[1. Fantasy.]   I. Krush, Beth, ill. II. Krush, Joe, ill. III. Title.
PZ7.N8248Bl 1986   [Fic]   86-4613

Printed in the United States of America
V X Z AA Y W
E G I J H F (pb)

For Peter and Caroline

THE BORROWERS AFLOAT

Chapter One

"But what do they talk about?" asked Mr. Beguid, the lawyer. He spoke almost irritably, as of foolish goings-on.

"They talk about the borrowers," said Mrs. May.

They stood beneath the shelter of the hedge among wet, treelike cabbages, which tumbled in the wind. Below them on this dark, dank afternoon, a lamp glowed warmly through the cottage window. "We could have an orchard here," she added lightly, as though to change the subject.

"At our time of life," remarked Mr. Beguid, gazing still at the lighted window below them in the hollow, "yours and mine—it's wiser to plant flowers than fruit . . ."

"You think so?" said Mrs. May. She drew her ulster cape about her against the eddying wind. "But I'll leave her the cottage, you see, in my will."

"Leave whom the cottage?"

"Kate, my niece."

"I see," said Mr. Beguid, and he glanced again toward the lighted window behind which he knew Kate was sitting: a strange child, he thought; disconcerting—the way she gazed through one with wide unseeing eyes and yet would chatter by the hour with old Tom Goodenough, a rascally one-time gamekeeper. What could they have in common, he asked himself, this sly old man and eager, listening child? There they had been now (he glanced at his watch) for a good hour and a quarter, hunched by the window, talking, talking . . .

"Borrowers . . ." he repeated, as though troubled by the word. "What kind of borrowers?"

"Oh, it's just a story," said Mrs. May lightly, picking her way amongst the rain-drenched cabbages toward the raised brick path, "something we used to tell each other, my brother and I, when we stayed down here as children."

"At Firbank Hall, you mean?"

"Yes, with Great-Aunt Sophy. Kate loves this story."

"But why," asked Mr. Beguid, "should she want to tell it to him?"

"To old Tom? Why not? As a matter of fact, I believe it's the other way round: I believe he tells it to her."

As he followed Mrs. May along the worn brick path, Mr. Beguid became silent. He had known this family most of his life, and a strange lot (he had begun to think lately) they were.

"But a story made up by you?"

"Not by me, no—" Mrs. May laughed as though embarrassed. "It was my brother, I think, who made it up. If it was made up," she added suddenly, just above her breath.

Mr. Beguid pounced on the words. "I don't quite follow you. This story you speak of, is it something that actually happened?"

Mrs. May laughed. "Oh no, it couldn't have actually happened. Not possibly." She began to walk on again, adding over her shoulder, "It's just that this old man, this old Tom Goodenough, seems to know about these people."

"What people? These cadgers?"

"Not cadgers—borrowers . . ."

"I see," said Mr. Beguid, who didn't see at all.

"We called them that," and turning on the path, she waited for him to catch up with her. "Or rather they called themselves that—because they had nothing of their own at all. Even their names were borrowed. The family we knew—father, mother, and child—were called Pod, Homily and little Arrietty." As he came beside her, she smiled. "I think their names are rather charming."

"Very," he said, a little too drily. And then, in spite of himself, he smiled back at her. Always, he remembered, there had been in her manner this air of gentle mockery; even as a young man, though attracted by her prettiness, he had found her disconcerting. "You haven't changed," he said.

She at once became more serious. "But you can't deny that it was a strange old house?"

"Old, yes. But no more strange than"—he looked down the slope—"than this cottage, say."

Mrs. May laughed. "Ah, there Kate would agree with you! She finds this cottage quite as strange as we found Firbank, neither more nor less. You know, at Firbank, my brother and I—right from the very first—had this feeling that there were other people living in the house besides the human beings."

"But—" exclaimed Mr. Beguid, exasperated, "there can be no such thing as 'people' other than human beings. The terms are synonymous."

"Other personalities, then. Something far smaller than a human being but like them in essentials—a little larger-seeming in the head, perhaps, a little longer in the hands and feet. But very small and hidden. We imagined that they lived like mice—in the wainscots, or behind the skirtings, or under the floorboards—and were entirely dependent on what they could filch from the great house above. Yet you couldn't call it stealing: it was more a kind of garnering. On the whole, they only took things that could well be spared."

"What sort of things?" asked Mr. Beguid. Suddenly feeling foolish, he sprang ahead of her to clear a trail of bramble from her path.

"Oh, all sorts of things. Any kind of food, of course, and any other small movable objects which might be useful—matchboxes, pencil ends, needles, bits of stuff—anything they could turn into tools or clothes or furniture. It was rather sad for them, we thought, because they had a sort of longing for beauty and for making their dark little holes as charming and comfortable as the homes of human beings. My brother used to help them"—Mrs. May hesitated suddenly as though embarrassed—"or so he said," she concluded lamely, and she gave a little laugh.

"I see," said Mr. Beguid again. He became silent as they skirted the side of the cottage to avoid the dripping thatch. "And where does Tom Goodenough come in?" he asked at last as she paused beside the water butt.

She turned to face him. "Well, it's extraordinary, isn't it? At my age—nearly seventy—to inherit this cottage and find him still here in possession?"

"Not in possession, exactly—he's the outgoing tenant."

"I mean," said Mrs. May, "to find him here at all. In the old days, when they were boys, he and my brother used to go rabbiting—in a way they were great companions. But that all ended—after the rumpus."

"Oh," said Mr. Beguid, "so there was a rumpus?" They stood together by the weatherworn front door, and intrigued against his wish, he withdrew his hand from the latch.

"There most certainly was," exclaimed Mrs. May. "I should have thought you might have heard about it. Even the policeman was implicated—you remember Ernie Runacre? It must have gone all over the village. The cook and the gardener got wind of these creatures and determined to smoke them out. They got in the local ratcatcher and sent up here for Tom to bring his ferret. He was a boy then, the gamekeeper's grandson—a little older than we were, but still quite young. But"—Mrs. May turned suddenly toward him—"you *must* have heard something of this?"

Mr. Beguid frowned. Past rumors stirred vaguely in his memory . . . some nonsense or other at Firbank Hall; a cook with a name like Diver or Driver; things missing from the cabinet in the drawing room . . .

"Wasn't there"—he said at last—"some trouble about an emerald watch?"

"Yes, that's why they sent for the police."

"But"—Mr. Beguid's frown deepened—"this woman, Diver or—"

"Driver! Yes, that was the name."

"And this gardener—you mean to say they believed in these creatures?"

"Obviously," said Mrs. May, "or they would not have made all this fuss."

"What happened?" asked Mr. Beguid. "Did they catch them? No, no—I don't mean that! What I meant to say is—what did they turn out to be? Mice, I suppose?"

"I wasn't there myself at the time—so I can't say 'what they turned out to be.' But according to my brother, they escaped out of doors through a grating just in the nick of time: one of those ventilator things set low down in the brickwork outside. They ran away across the orchard and"—she looked around her in the half light—"up into these fields."

"Were they seen to go?"

"No," said Mrs. May.

Mr. Beguid glanced swiftly down the mist-enshrouded slopes. Against the pallid fields the woods beyond looked dark—already wrapped in twilight.

"Squirrels," he said, "that's what they were, most likely."

"Possibly," said Mrs. May. She moved away from him to where, beside the washhouse, the workmen that morning had opened up a drain. "Wouldn't this be wide enough to take sewage?"

"Wide enough, yes," said Mr. Beguid, "but the sanitary inspector would never allow it: all these drains flow into the stream. No, you'll have to have a septic tank, I'm afraid."

"Then what was this used for?"

He nodded toward the washhouse. "The overflow from the sink." He glanced at his watch. "Could I give you a lift anywhere? It's getting rather late . . ."

"That's very kind of you," said Mrs. May as they moved toward the front door.

"An odd story," remarked Mr. Beguid, putting his hand to the latch.

"Yes, very odd."

"I mean—to go to the lengths of sending for the police. Extraordinary."

"Yes," agreed Mrs. May, and paused to wipe her feet on a piece of torn sacking that lay beside the step.

Mr. Beguid glanced at his own shoes and followed her example. "Your brother must have been very convincing."

"Yes, he was."

"And very inventive."

"Yes, according to my brother there was quite a colony of these people. He talked about another lot, cousins of the ones at Firbank, who were supposed to live in a badger's set—up here on the edge of these woods. Uncle Hendreary and Aunt Lupy . . ." She looked at him sideways. "This lot had four children."

"According to your brother," remarked Mr. Beguid, as he reached again for the latch.

"And according to old Tom—" She laughed and lowered her voice. "Old Tom swears that the story is true. But *he* contends that they did not live in the badger's set at all; or that, if they did, it could not have been for long. He insists that for years and years they lived up here, in the lath and plaster beside the fireplace."

"Which fireplace?" asked Mr. Beguid uneasily.

"This fireplace," said Mrs. May. As the door swung open, she dropped her voice to a whisper. "Here in this very cottage."

"Here in this very cottage . . ." repeated Mr. Beguid

in a startled voice, and standing aside for Mrs. May to pass, he craned his neck forward to peer within, without advancing across the threshold.

The quiet room seemed empty: all they could see at first was yellow lamplight spilling across the flagstones and dying embers in the grate. By the window stood a stack of hazel wands, split and trimmed for thatching, beyond them a wooden armchair. Then Kate emerged rather suddenly from the shadows beside the fireplace. "Hullo," she said.

She seemed about to say more, but her gaze slid past Mrs. May to where Mr. Beguid hovered in the doorway. "I was looking up the chimney," she explained.

"So I see—your face is black!"

"Is it?" said Kate, without interest. Her eyes looked very bright and she seemed to be waiting—either, thought Mrs. May, for Mr. Beguid to shut the door and come in or for Mr. Beguid to shut the door and depart.

Mrs. May glanced at the empty armchair and then past Kate toward the door of the washhouse. "Where's Tom?"

"Gone out to feed the pig," said Kate. Again she hesitated, then, in a burst, she added, "Need we go yet? It's only a step across the fields, and there's something I terribly want to show you—"

Mr. Beguid glanced at his watch. "Well, in that case—" he began.

"Yes, please don't wait for us," interrupted Mrs. May

impulsively. "As Kate says, it's only a step . . ."

"I was only going to say," continued Mr. Beguid stolidly from his neutral position on the threshold, "that as this lane's so narrow and the ditches so full of mud, I propose to drive on ahead and turn the car at the crossroads." He began to button up his overcoat. "Perhaps you would listen for the horn?"

"Yes, yes, indeed. Thank you . . . of course. We'll be listening . . ."

When the front door had closed and Mr. Beguid had gone, Kate took Mrs. May by the hand and drew her urgently toward the fireplace. "And I've heaps to tell you. Heaps and heaps . . ."

"We weren't rude, were we?" asked Mrs. May. "I mean to Mr. Beguid? We didn't shoo him off?"

"No, no, of course not. You thanked him beautifully. But look—" Kate went on. "Please look!" Loosing Mrs. May's hand, she ran forward and—with much tugging and panting—dragged out the log box from where it was jammed against the wall beside the hearth. A rat hole was revealed in the skirting—slightly Gothic in shape. "That's where they lived—" cried Kate.

Mrs. May, in spite of herself, felt a curious sense of shock; staring down at it, she said uneasily, "We mustn't be too credulous, Kate. I mean, we can't believe *quite* everything we hear. And you know what they say about old Tom?"

"In the village? Yes, I know what they say—'the big-

gest liar in five counties.' But all that started *because* of the
borrowers. At first, you see, he used to talk about them.
And that was his mistake. He thought people would be
interested. But they weren't interested—not at all: they
just didn't believe him." Kate knelt down on the hearth,
and breathing rather heavily, she peered into the darkness of the hole. "There was only one other human being, I think, who really believed in the borrowers. . . ."

"Mrs. Driver, you mean, the cook at Firbank?"

Kate frowned, sitting back on her heels. "No, I don't
really think that Mrs. Driver *did* believe in them. She saw
them, I know, but I don't think she trusted her eyes. No,
the one I was thinking of was Mild Eye, the gypsy. I
mean, he actually shook them out of his boot onto the
floor of his caravan. And there they were—right under

his nose—and no two ways about it. He tried to grab them, Tom says, but they got away. He wanted to put them in a cage and show them for pennies at the fair. It was Tom who rescued them. With the help of Spiller, of course."

"Who was Spiller?" asked Mrs. May—she still stared, as though spellbound, at the rat hole. Kate seemed amazed. "You haven't heard of Spiller?"

"No," said Mrs. May.

"Oh," cried Kate, throwing her head back and half closing her eyes, "Spiller was wonderful!"

"I am sure he was," said Mrs. May. She pulled forward a rush-seated chair and rather stiffly sat down on it. "But you and Tom have been talking for days, remember. . . . I'm a little out of touch. What was Spiller supposed to be —a borrower?"

"He *was* a borrower," corrected Kate, "but rather on the wild side—he lived in the hedgerows, and wore old moleskins, and didn't really wash. . . ."

"He doesn't sound so *tremendously* wonderful."

"Oh, but he was: Spiller ran for Tom and Tom rushed down and rescued them; he snatched them up from under the gypsies' noses and pushed them into his pockets; he brought them up here—all four of them—Spiller, Pod, Homily, and Arrietty. And he set them down very carefully, one by one"—Kate patted the warm flagstones— "here, on this very spot. And then, poor things, they ran away into the wall through that rat hole in the skirting"

—Kate lowered her head again, trying to peer in—"and up a tiny ladder just inside to where the cousins were living. . . ." She scrambled up suddenly and, stretching one arm as far as it would go, she tapped on the plaster beside the chimney. "The cousins' house was somewhere up here. Quite high. Two floors they had—between the lath and plaster of the washhouse wall and the lath and plaster of this one. They used the chimney, Tom says, and they tapped the washhouse pipes for water. Arrietty didn't like it up there: she used to creep down in the evenings and talk to young Tom. But our lot did not stay there long. Something happened, you see—"

"Tell me," said Mrs. May.

"Well, there isn't really time now. Mr. Beguid will start hooting. . . . And old Tom's the one to tell it: he seems to know everything—even what they said and did when no one else was there. . . ."

"He's a born storyteller, that's why," said Mrs. May, laughing. "And he knows people. Given a struggle for life, people react very much alike—according to type, of course—whatever their size or station." Mrs. May leaned forward as though to examine the skirting. "Even I," she said, "can imagine what Homily felt, homeless and destitute, faced with that dusty hole. . . . And strange relations living up above who didn't know she was coming and whom she hadn't seen for years . . ."

Chapter Two

But Mrs. May was not quite right: she had underestimated their sudden sense of security—the natural joy a borrower feels when safely under cover. It is true that, as they filed in through the Gothic-shaped hole in the skirting, they had felt a little nervous, a little forlorn; this was because, at first glance, the cavelike space about them seemed disappointingly uninhabited: empty, dark and echoing, it smelled of dust and mice. . . .

"Oh, dear," Homily had muttered incredulously, "they can't live here!" But as her eyes became used to the dimness, she had stooped suddenly to pick up some object from the floor. "My goodness," she whispered excitedly to Pod, "do you know what this is?"

"Yes," Pod had told her. "It's a bit of quill pipe-cleaner. Put it down, Homily, and come on, do. Spiller's waiting."

"It's the spout of our old oak-apple teapot," Homily had persisted. "I'd know it anywhere and it's no good telling me any different. So they *are* here . . ." she mused wonderingly as she followed Pod into the shadows, ". . .

and from somewhere, somehow, they've got hold of some of our things."

"We go up here," said Spiller, and Homily saw that he stood with his hand on a ladder. Glancing up to where the rungs soared away above them into dimness, she gave a slight shudder. The ladder was made of matchsticks, neatly glued and spliced to two lengths of split cane such as florists use to support potted plants.

"I'll go first," said Pod. "We better take it one at a time."

Homily watched fearfully until she heard his voice from above.

"It's all right," he whispered from some invisible eyrie. "Come on up."

Homily followed, her knees trembling, and emerged at last onto the dim-lit platform beside Pod—an aerial landing stage, that was what it seemed like—which creaked a little when she stepped on it and almost seemed to sway. Below lay hollow darkness, ahead an open door. "Oh, my goodness," she muttered, "I do hope it's safe. . . . Don't look down," she advised Arrietty, who came up next.

But Arrietty had no temptation to look down: her eyes were on the lighted doorway and the moving shadows within; she heard the faint sound of voices and a sudden high-pitched laugh.

"Come on," said Spiller, slipping past and making toward the door.

Arrietty never forgot her first sight of that upstairs room: the warmth, the sudden cleanliness, the winking candlelight, and the smell of home-cooked food.

And so many voices . . . so many people . . .

Gradually, in a dazed way, she began to sort them out. That must be Aunt Lupy embracing her mother—Aunt Lupy so round and glowing, her mother so smudged and lean. Why did they cling and weep, she wondered, and squeeze each other's hands? They had never liked each other—all the world knew that. Homily had thought Lupy stuck-up because, back in the big house, Lupy had lived in the drawing room and (she had heard it rumored) changed for dinner at night. And Lupy despised Homily for living under the kitchen and for pronouncing parquet "parkett."

And here was Uncle Hendreary, his beard grown thinner, telling her father that this could not be Arrietty, and her father, with pride, telling Uncle Hendreary it could. Those must be the three boy cousins—whose names she had not caught—graduated in size but as like as peas in a pod. And this thin, tall, fairylike creature, neither old nor young, who hovered shyly in the background with a faint uneasy smile, who was she? Could it be Eggletina? Yes, she supposed it could.

And there was something strangely unreal about the room—furnished with dollhouse furniture of every shape and size, none of it matching or in proportion. There were chairs upholstered in rep or velvet, some of them too small to sit in and some too steep and large; there were chiffoniers that were too tall and occasional tables far too low; and a toy fireplace with colored plaster coals and its fire irons stuck down all-of-a-piece with the fender; there were two make-believe windows with curved pelmets and red satin curtains, each hand-painted with an imitation view—one looked out on a Swiss mountain scene, the other on a Highland glen ("Eggletina did them," Aunt Lupy boasted in her rich society voice. "We're going to have a third when we get the curtains—a view of Lake Como from Monte S. Primo"); there were table lamps and standard lamps, flounced, festooned, and tasseled, but the light in the room, Arrietty noticed, came from humble dips like those they had made at home.

Everybody looked extraordinarily clean, and Arrietty became even shier. She threw a quick glance at her father and mother and was not reassured: none of their clothes had been washed for weeks nor, for some days, had their hands and faces. Pod's trousers had a tear in one knee and Homily's hair hung down in snakes. And here was Aunt Lupy, plump and polite, begging Homily please to take off her things in the kind of voice, Arrietty imagined, usually reserved for feather boas, opera cloaks, and freshly cleaned kid gloves.

"Poor dear Lupy," Homily was saying, glancing wearily about, "what a lot of furniture! Whoever helps you with the dusting?" And swaying a little, she sank on a chair.

They rushed to support her, as she hoped they might. Water was brought and they bathed her face and hands. Hendreary stood with the tears in his brotherly eyes. "Poor valiant soul," he muttered, shaking his head. "Your mind kind of reels when you think of what she's been through. . . ."

Then, after a quick wash and brush up all round and a brisk bit of eye-wiping, they all sat down to supper. This they ate in the kitchen, which was rather a comedown except that, in here, the fire was real: a splendid cooking-range made of a large, black door-lock; they poked the fire through the keyhole, which glowed handsomely, and the smoke, they were told, went out through a series of pipes to the cottage chimney behind.

The long, white table was richly spread: it was an eighteenth-century finger-plate off some old drawing-room door—white-enameled and painted with forget-me-nots—supported firmly on four stout pencil stubs where once the screws had been; the points of the pencils emerged slightly through the top of the table; one was copying ink, and they were warned not to touch it in case it stained their hands.

There was every kind of dish and preserve—both real and false; pies, puddings, and bottled fruits out of season —all cooked by Lupy, and an imitation leg of mutton and a dish of plaster tarts borrowed from the dollhouse. There were three real tumblers as well as acorn cups and a couple of green glass decanters.

Talk, talk, talk. . . . Arrietty, listening, felt dazed. "Where is Spiller?" she asked suddenly.

"Oh, he's gone off," said Hendreary vaguely. He seemed a little embarrassed and sat there frowning and tapping the table with a pewter spoon (one of a set of six, Homily remembered angrily; she wondered how many were left).

"Gone off where?" asked Arrietty.

"Home, I reckon," Hendreary told her.

"But we haven't thanked him," cried Arrietty. "Spiller saved our lives!"

Hendreary threw off his gloom. "Have a drop of blackberry cordial," he suggested suddenly to Pod. "Lupy's own make. Cheer us all up. . . ."

"Not for me," said Homily firmly, before Pod could speak. "No good never comes of it, as we've found out to our cost."

"We haven't even thanked him," persisted Arrietty, and there were tears in her eyes.

Hendreary looked at her, surprised. "Spiller? He don't hold with thanks. He's all right . . ." and he patted Arrietty's arm.

"Why didn't he stay for supper?"

"He don't ever," Hendreary told her. "Doesn't like company. He'll cook something on his own."

"Where?"

"In his stove."

"But that's miles away!"

"Not for Spiller—he's used to it. Goes part way by water."

"And it must be getting dark," Arrietty went on unhappily.

"Now don't you fret about Spiller," her uncle told her. "You eat up your pie. . . ."

Arrietty looked down at her plate (pink celluloid, it was, part of a tea service that she seemed to remember); somehow she had no appetite. She raised her eyes. "And when will he be back?" she asked anxiously.

"He don't come back much. Once a year for his new clothes. Or if young Tom sends 'im special."

Arrietty looked thoughtful. "He must be lonely," she ventured at last.

"Spiller? No, I wouldn't say he was lonely. Some borrowers is made like that. Solitary. You get 'em now and again." He glanced across the room to where his daughter, having left the table, was sitting alone by the fire. "Eggletina's a bit like that. . . . Pity, but you can't do nothing about it. Them's the ones as gets this craze for humans—kind of man-eaters, they turns out to be. . . ."

Very dark it was, this strange new home, almost as dark as under the floorboards at Firbank, and lit by wax dips fixed to upturned drawing pins (how many human dwellings must be burned down, Arrietty realized suddenly, through the carelessness of borrowers running about with lighted candles). In spite of Lupy's polishings, the compartments smelled of soot and always in the background a pervading odor of cheese.

The cousins all slept in the kitchen—for warmth, Lupy explained. The ornate drawing room was only rarely used. Outside the drawing room was the shadowed platform with its perilous matchstick ladder leading down below.

Above this landing, high among the shadows, were the two small rooms allotted them by Lupy. There was no way up to them as yet, except by climbing hand over hand from lath to lath and scrabbling blindly for footholds, to emerge at length on a rough piece of flooring made by Hendreary from the lid of a cardboard shoe box.

"Do those rooms good to be used," Lupy had said (she knew Pod was a handyman), "and we'll lend you furniture to start with."

"To start with," muttered Homily that first morning as, foot after hand, she followed Pod up the laths. Unlike most borrowers, she was not very fond of climbing. "What are we meant to do after?"

She dared not look down. Beneath her, she knew, was the rickety platform below which again were further depths and the matchstick ladder gleaming like a fishbone. "Anyway," she comforted herself, feeling clumsily for footholds, "steep it may be, but at least it's a separate entrance. . . . What's it like, Pod?" she asked as her head emerged suddenly at floor level through the circular trap door—very startling it looked, as though decapitated.

"It's dry," said Pod, noncommittally; he stamped about a bit on the floor as though to test it.

"Don't stamp so, Pod," Homily complained, seeking a foothold on the quivering surface. "It's only cardboard."

"I know," said Pod. "Mustn't grumble," he added as Homily came toward him.

"At least," said Homily, looking about her, "back home under the kitchen, we was on solid ground. . . ."

"You've lived in a boot since," Pod reminded her, "and you've lived in a hole in a bank. And nearly starved. And nearly frozen. And nearly been captured by the gypsies. Mustn't grumble," he said again.

Homily looked about her. Two rooms? They were barely that: a sheet of cardboard between two sets of laths, divided by a cloth-covered book cover, on which the words "Pig Breeders' Annual, 1896" were stamped in tarnished gold. In this dark purple wall, Hendreary had cut a door. Ceilings there were none, and an eerie light came down from somewhere far above—a crack, Homily supposed, between the floorboards and the whitewashed walls of the gamekeeper's bedroom.

"Who sleeps up there," she asked Pod. "That boy's father?"

"Grandfather," said Pod.

"He'll be after us, I shouldn't wonder," said Homily, "with traps and what-not."

"Yes, you've got to be quiet," said Pod, "especially

with gamekeepers. Out most of the day, though, and the young boy with him. Yes, it's dry," he repeated, looking about him, "and warm."

"Not very," said Homily. As she followed him through the doorway, she saw that the door was hung by the canvas binding that Hendreary had not cut through. "Soon fray, that will," she remarked, swinging the panel to and fro, "and then what?"

"I can stitch it," said Pod, "with me cobbler's thread. Easy." He laid his hands on the great stones of the farther wall. "'Tis the chimney casing," he explained. "Warm, eh?"

"Um," said Homily, "if you lean against it."

"What about if we sleep here—right against the chimney?"

"What in?" asked Homily.

"They're going to lend us beds."

"No, better keep the chimney for cooking." Homily ran her hands across the stones and from a vertical crevice began to pick out the plaster. "Soon get through here to the main flue. . . ."

"But we're going to eat downstairs with them," Pod explained. "That's what's been arranged—so that it's all one cooking."

"All one cooking and all one borrowing," said Homily. "There won't be no borrowing for you, Pod."

"Rubbish," said Pod. "Whatever makes you say a thing like that?"

"Because," explained Homily, "in a cottage like this with only two human beings, a man and a boy, there aren't the pickings there were back at Firbank. You mark my words: I been talking to Lupy. Hendreary and the two elder boys can manage the lot. They won't be wanting competition."

"Then what'll I do?" said Pod. A borrower deprived of borrowing—especially a borrower of Pod's standing? His eyes became round and blank.

"Get on with the furniture, I suppose."

"But they're going to lend us that."

"Lend us!" hissed Homily. "Everything they've got was ours!"

"Now, Homily—" began Pod.

Homily dropped her voice, speaking in a breathless whisper. "Every single blessed thing. That red velvet chair, the dresser with the painted plates, all that stuff the boy brought us from the dollhouse . . ."

"Not the keyhole stove," put in Pod, "not that dining table they've made from a doorplate. Not the—"

"The imitation leg of mutton, that was ours," interrupted Homily, "and the dish of plaster tarts. All the beds were ours, and the sofa. And the palm in a pot. . . . *And* they got your hatpin, over behind the stove. Been poking the fire with it most likely. I wouldn't put it past them. . . ."

"Now listen, Homily," pleaded Pod, "we've been into all that, remember. I'll take back the hatpin—that I will take—but findings keepings, as they say. Far as they knew we was dead and gone—like as we might be lost at sea. The things all came to them in a plain white pillowcase delivered to the door. See what I mean? It's like as if they was left them in a will."

"I would never have left anything to Lupy," remarked Homily.

"Now, Homily, you've got to say they've been kind."

"Yes," agreed Homily, "you've got to say it."

Unhappily she gazed about her. The cardboard floor was scattered with lumps of fallen plaster. Absent-mindedly she began to push these toward the gaps where the floor, being straight-edged, did not fit against the rough plaster. They clattered hollowly down the hidden shaft into Lupy's kitchen.

"Now you've done it," said Pod. "And that's the kind of noise we mustn't make, not if we value our lives. To human beings," he went on, "droppings and rollings means rats or squirrels. You know that as well as I do."

"Sorry," said Homily.

"Wait a minute," said Pod. He had been gazing upwards toward the crack of light, and now in a flash he was on the laths and climbing up toward it.

"Careful, Pod," whispered Homily. He seemed to be pulling at some object that was hidden from Homily by the line of his body. She heard him grunting with the effort.

"It's all right," said Pod in his normal voice, beginning

to climb down again. "There isn't no one up there. Here you are," he went on as he landed on the floor and handed her an old bone toothbrush, slightly taller than herself. "The first borrowing," he announced modestly, and she saw that he was pleased. "Someone must have dropped it up there in the bedroom, and it wedged itself in this crack between the floorboards and the wall. We can borrow from up there," he went on, "easy; the wall's fallen away like or the floorboards have shrunk. Farther along it gets even wider. . . . And here you are again," he said and handed her a fair-sized cockleshell he had pulled out from the rough plaster. "You go on sweeping," he told her, "and I'll pop up again, might as well, while it's free of human beings. . . ."

"Now, Pod, go careful . . ." Homily urged him, with a mixture of pride and anxiety. She watched him climb the laths and watched him disappear before, using the cockleshell as a dustpan, she began to sweep the floor. When Arrietty arrived to tell them a meal was ready, a fair-sized haul was laid out on the floor; the bottom of a china soap dish for baths, a crocheted table mat in red and yellow that would do as a carpet, a worn sliver of pale green soap with gray veins in it, a large darning needle—slightly rusted—three aspirin tablets, a packet of pipe cleaners, and a fair length of tarred string.

"I'm kind of hungry," said Pod.

Chapter Three

They climbed down the laths onto the platform, keeping well away from the edge, through Lupy's drawing room, into the kitchen.

"Ah, here you are," cried Lupy, in her loud, rich, aunt-like voice—very plump she looked in her dress of purple silk, and flushed from the heat of the stove. Homily, beside her, looked as thin and angular as a clothes peg. "We were just going to start without you."

The doorplate table was lit by a single lamp; it was made from a silver salt shaker with a hole in the top, out of which protruded a wick. The flame burned stilly in that airless room, and the porcelain table top, icily white, swam in a sea of shadow.

Eggletina, by the stove, was ladling out soup, which Timmus, the younger boy, unsteadily carried round in yellow snail shells—very pretty they looked, scoured and polished. They were rather alike—Eggletina and Timmus —Arrietty thought, quiet and pale and watchful-seeming.

Hendreary and the two elder boys were already seated, tucking into their food.

"Get up, get up," cried Lupy archly, "when your aunt comes in," and her two elder sons rose reluctantly and quickly sat down again. "Harpsichord manners . . ." their expressions seemed to say. They were too young to remember those gracious days in the drawing room of the big house—the Madeira cake, little sips of China tea, and music of an evening. Churlish and shy, they hardly ever spoke. "They don't much like us," Arrietty decided as she took her place at the table. Little Timmus, his hands in a cloth, brought her a shell of soup. The thin shell was piping hot, and she found it hard to hold.

It was a plain meal, but wholesome: soup, and boiled butter beans with a trace of dripping—one bean each. There was none of that first evening's lavishness when Lupy had raided her store cupboards. It was as though she and Hendreary had talked things over, setting more modest standards. "We must begin," she had imagined Lupy saying to Hendreary in a firm, self-righteous voice, "as we mean to go on."

There was, however, a sparrow's egg omelette, fried in a tin lid, for Hendreary and the two boys. Lupy saw to it herself. Seasoned with thyme and a trace of wild garlic, it smelled very savory and sizzled on the plate. "They've been borrowing, you see," Lupy explained, "out of doors all morning. They can only get out when the front door's

open, and on some days they can't get back. Three nights Hendreary spent once in the woodshed before he got his chance."

Homily glanced at Pod, who had finished his bean and whose eyes had become strangely round. "Pod's done a bit, too, this morning," she remarked carelessly, "more high than far; but it does give you an appetite. . . ."

"Borrowing?" asked Uncle Hendreary. He seemed amazed, and his thin beard had ceased the up-and-down movement that went with his eating.

"One or two things," said Pod modestly.

"From where?" asked Hendreary, staring.

"The old man's bedroom. It's just above us. . . ."

Hendreary was silent a moment and then he said, "That's all right, Pod," but as though it wasn't all right at all. "But we've got to go steady. There isn't much in this house, not to spare like. We can't all go at it like bulls at gates." He took another mouthful of omelette and consumed it slowly while Arrietty, fascinated, watched his beard and the shadow it threw on the wall. When he had swallowed, he said, "I'd take it as a favor, Pod, if you'd just leave borrowing for a while. We know the territory, as you might say, and we work to our own methods. Better we lend you things, for the time being. And there's food for all, if you don't mind it plain."

There was a long silence. The two elder boys, Arrietty noticed, shoveling up their food, kept their eyes on their plates. Lupy clattered about at the stove. Eggletina sat looking at her hands, and little Timmus stared wonderingly from one to another, eyes wide in his small pale face.

"As you wish," said Pod slowly, as Lupy bustled back to the table.

"Homily," said Lupy brightly, breaking the awkward silence, "this afternoon, if you've got a moment to spare, I'd be much obliged if you'd give me a hand with Spiller's summer clothes. . . ."

Homily thought of the comfortless rooms upstairs and of all she longed to do to them. "But of course," she told Lupy, trying to smile.

"I always get them finished," Lupy explained, "by early spring. Time's getting on now: the hawthorn's out—or so they tell me." And she began to clear the table; they all jumped up to help her.

"Where *is* Spiller?" asked Homily, trying to stack the snail shells.

"Goodness knows," said Lupy, "off on some wild goose chase. No one knows where Spiller is. Nor what he does for that matter. All I know is," she went on, taking the plug out of the pipe (as they used to do at home Arrietty remembered) to release a trickle of water, "that I make his moleskin suits each autumn and his white kid ones each spring and that he always comes to fetch them."

"It's very kind of you to make his suits," said Arrietty, watching Lupy rinse the snail shells in a small crystal salt cellar and standing by to dry them.

"It's only human," said Lupy.

"Human!" exclaimed Homily, startled by the choice of word.

"Human—just short like that—means kind," explained Lupy, remembering that Homily, poor dear, had had no education, being dragged up as you might say under a kitchen floor. "It's got nothing at all to do with human beings. How could it have?"

"That's what I was wondering . . ." said Homily.

"Besides," Lupy went on, "he brings us things in exchange."

"Oh, I see," said Homily.

"He goes hunting, you see, and I smoke his meat for him—there in the chimney. Some we keep and some he takes away. What's over I make into paste with butter on the top—keeps for months that way. Birds' eggs, he brings, and berries and nuts . . . fish from the stream. I smoke the fish, too, or pickle it. Some things I put down in salt. . . . And if you want anything special, you tell Spiller—ahead of time, of course—and he borrows it from the gypsies. That old stove he lives in is just by their camping site. Give him time and he can get almost anything you want from the gypsies. We have a whole arm of a waterproof raincoat, got by Spiller, and very useful it was when the bees swarmed one summer—we all crawled inside it."

"What bees?" asked Homily.

"Haven't I told you about the bees in the thatch?

43

They've gone now. But that's how we got the honey, all we'd ever want, and a good, lasting wax for the candles. . . ."

Homily was silent a moment—enviously silent, dazzled by Lupy's riches. Then she said, as she stacked up the last snail shell, "Where do these go, Lupy?"

"Into that wickerwork hair-tidy in the corner. They won't break—just take them on the tin lid and drop them in. . . ."

"I must say, Lupy," Homily remarked wonderingly as she dropped the shells one by one into the hair-tidy (it was horn-shaped with a loop to hang it on and a faded blue bow on the top), "that you've become what I'd call a very good manager. . . ."

"For one," agreed Lupy, laughing, "who was brought up in a drawing room and never raised a hand."

"You weren't *brought up* in a drawing room," Homily reminded her.

"Oh, I don't remember those Rain-pipe days," said Lupy blithely. "I married so young. Just a child . . ." and she turned suddenly to Arrietty. "Now, what are you dreaming about, Miss-butter-wouldn't-melt-in-her-mouth?"

"I was thinking of Spiller," said Arrietty.

"A-ha!" cried Aunt Lupy. "She was thinking of Spiller!" And she laughed again. "You don't want to waste precious thoughts on a ragamuffin like Spiller. You'll meet lots of nice borrowers, all in good time. Maybe, one day, you'll meet one brought up in a library: they're the best, so they say, gentlemen all, and a good cultural background."

"I was thinking," continued Arrietty evenly, trying to keep her temper, "that I couldn't imagine Spiller dressed up in white kid."

"It doesn't stay white long," cried Lupy. "Of that I can assure you! It has to be white to start with because it's made from an evening glove. A ball glove, shoulder length—it's one of the few things I salvaged from the drawing room. But he will have kid, says it's hard-wearing. It stiffens up, of course, directly he gets it wet, but he soon wears it soft again. And by that time," she added, "it's all colors of the rainbow."

Arrietty could imagine the colors; they would not be "all colors of the rainbow"; they would be colors without real color, the shades that made Spiller invisible—soft fawns, pale browns, dull greens, and a kind of shadowy gun-metal. Spiller took care about "seasoning" his clothes: he brought them to a stage where he could melt into the landscape, where one could stand beside him, almost within touching distance, and yet not see him. Spiller deceived animals as well as gypsies. Spiller deceived hawks, and stoats, and foxes. . . . Spiller might not wash but he had no Spiller scent: he smelled of hedgerows, and bark, and grasses, and of wet sun-warmed earth; he smelled of buttercups, dried cow dung, and early morning dew. . . .

"When will he come?" Arrietty asked, but ran away upstairs before anyone could tell her. She wept a little in the upstairs room, crouched beside the soap dish.

To talk of Spiller reminded her of out-of-doors and of a wild, free life she might never know again. This new-found haven among the lath and plaster had all too soon become another prison. . . .

Chapter Four

It was Hendreary and the boys who carried the furniture up the laths with Pod standing by to receive it. In this way, Lupy lent them just what she wished to lend and nothing they would have chosen. Homily did not grumble, however. She had become very quiet lately as slowly she realized their position.

Sometimes they stayed downstairs after meals, helping generally or talking to Lupy. But they gauged the length of these visits according to Lupy's mood: when she became flustered, blaming them for some small mishap brought on by herself, they knew it was time to go. "We couldn't do right today," they would say, sitting empty-handed upstairs on Homily's old champagne corks that Lupy had unearthed for stools. They would sit by the chimney casing in the inner room to get the heat from the stones. Here Pod and Homily had a double bed, one of those from the dollhouse. Arrietty slept in the outer room, close beside the entrance hole. She slept on a thickish piece of wadding, borrowed in the old days from a box of artist's pastels, and they had given her most of the bedclothes.

"We shouldn't have come, Pod," Homily said one evening as they sat alone upstairs.

"We had no choice," said Pod.

"And we got to go," she added and sat there watching him as he stitched the sole of a boot.

"To where?" asked Pod.

Things had become a little better for Pod lately: he had filed down the rusted needle and was back at his cobbling. Hendreary had brought him the skin of a weasel, one of those nailed up by the gamekeeper to dry on the outhouse door, and he was making them all new shoes. This pleased Lupy very much, and she had become a little less bossy.

"Where's Arrietty?" asked Homily one evening.

"Downstairs, I shouldn't wonder," said Pod.

"What does she do downstairs?"

"Tells Timmus a story and puts him to bed."

"I know that," said Homily, "but why does she stay so long? I'd nearly dropped off last night when we heard her come up the laths. . . ."

"I suppose they get talking," said Pod.

Homily was silent a moment and then she said, "I don't feel easy. I've got my feeling. . . ." This was the feeling borrowers get when human beings are near; with Homily it started at the knees.

Pod glanced up toward the floorboards above them

from whence came a haze of candlelight. "It's the old man going to bed."

"No," said Homily, getting up. "I'm used to that. We hear that every night." She began to walk about. "I think," she said at last, "that I'll just pop downstairs. . . ."

"What for?" asked Pod.

"To see if she's there."

"It's late," said Pod.

"All the more reason," said Homily.

"Where else would she be?" asked Pod.

"I don't know, Pod. I've got my feeling and I've had it once or twice lately," she said.

Homily had grown more used to the laths: she had become more agile, even in the dark. But tonight it was very dark indeed. When she reached the landing below, she felt a sense of yawning space and a kind of draft from the depth, which eddied hollowly around her: feeling her way to the drawing-room door, she kept well back from the edge of the platform.

The drawing room, too, was strangely dark and so was the kitchen beyond: there was a faint glow from the keyhole fire and a rhythmic sound of breathing.

"Arrietty?" she called softly from the doorway, just above a whisper.

Hendreary gave a snort and mumbled in his sleep: she heard him turning over.

"Arrietty . . ." whispered Homily again.

"What's that?" cried Lupy, suddenly and sharply.

"It's me . . . Homily."

"What do you want? We were all asleep. Hendreary's had a hard day. . . ."

"Nothing," faltered Homily, "it's all right. I was looking for Arrietty. . . ."

"Arrietty went upstairs hours ago," said Lupy.

"Oh," said Homily, and was silent a moment: the air was full of breathing. "All right," she said at last, "thank you . . . I'm sorry . . ."

"And shut the drawing-room door onto the landing as you go out. There's a howling draft," said Lupy.

As she felt her way back across the cluttered room, Homily saw a faint light ahead, a dim reflection from the landing. Could it come from above, she wondered, where Pod, two rooms away, was stitching? Yet it had not been there before. . . .

Fearfully she stepped out on the platform. The glow, she realized, did not come from above but from somewhere far below. The matchstick ladder was still in place, and she saw the top rungs quiver. After a moment's pause she summoned up the courage to peer over. Her startled eyes met those of Arrietty, who was climbing up the ladder and had nearly reached the top. Far below Homily could see the Gothic shape of the hole in the skirting: it seemed a blaze of light.

"Arrietty!" she gasped.

Arrietty did not speak. She climbed off the last rung of

the ladder, put her finger to her lips, and whispered. "I've got to draw it up. Move back." And Homily, as though in a trance, moved out of the way as Arrietty drew the ladder up rung over rung until it teetered above her into the darkness, and then, trembling a little with the effort, she eased it along and laid it against the laths.

"Well—" began Homily in a sort of gasp. In the half-light from below they could see each other's faces: Homily's aghast with her mouth hanging open; Arrietty's grave, her finger to her lips. "One minute," she whispered and went back to the edge. "All right," she called out softly into the space beneath; Homily heard a muffled thud, a scraping sound, the clap of wood on wood, and light below went out.

"He's pushed back the log box," Arrietty whispered across the sudden darkness. "Here, give me your hand. . . . Don't worry," she beseeched in a whisper, "and don't take on! I was going to tell you anyway." And supporting her shaking mother by the elbow, she helped her up the laths.

Pod looked up startled. "What's the matter?" he said as Homily sank down on the bed.

"Let me get her feet up first," said Arrietty. She did so gently and covered her mother's legs with a folded silk handkerchief, yellowed with washing and stained with marking ink, which Lupy had given them for a bedcover.

Homily lay with her eyes closed and spoke through pale lips. "She's been at it again," she said.

"At what?" asked Pod. He had laid down his boot and had risen to his feet.

"Talking to humans," said Homily.

Pod moved across and sat on the end of the bed. Homily opened her eyes. They both stared at Arrietty.

"Which ones?" asked Pod.

"Young Tom, of course," said Homily. "I caught her in the act. That's where she's been most evenings, I shouldn't wonder. Downstairs, they think she's up, and upstairs, we think she's down."

"Well, you know where that gets us," said Pod. He became very grave. "That, my girl, back at Firbank was the start of all our troubles."

"Talking to humans . . ." moaned Homily, and a quiver passed over her face. Suddenly she sat up on one elbow and glared at Arrietty. "You wicked, thoughtless girl, how *could* you do it again!"

Arrietty stared back at them, not defiantly exactly, but as though she were unimpressed. "But with this one downstairs," she protested, "I can't see why it matters. He knows we're here anyway, because he put us here himself! He could get at us any minute if he really wanted to. . . ."

"How could he get at us," said Homily, "right up here?"

"By breaking down the wall; it's only plaster."

"Don't say such things, Arrietty," shuddered Homily.

"But they're true," said Arrietty. "Anyway," she added, "he's going."

"Going?" said Pod sharply.

"They're both going," said Arrietty, "he and his grandfather; the grandfather's going to a place called Hospital, and the boy is going to a place called Leighton Buzzard to stay with his uncle who is an ostler. What's an ostler?" she asked.

But neither of her parents replied: they were staring blankly, struck dumb by a sudden thought.

"We've got to tell Hendreary," said Pod at last, "and quickly."

Homily nodded. She had swung her legs down from the bed.

"No good waking them now," said Pod. "I'll go down first thing in the morning."

"Oh, my goodness," breathed Homily, "all those poor children . . ."

"What's the matter?" asked Arrietty. "What have I said?" She felt scared suddenly and gazed uncertainly from one parent to the other.

"Arrietty," said Pod, turning toward her. His face had become very grave. "All we've told you about human beings is true; but what we haven't told you, or haven't stressed enough, is that we, the borrowers, cannot survive without them." He drew a long deep breath. "When they close up a house and go away, it usually means we're done for. . . ."

"No food, no fire, no clothes, no heat, no water . . ." chanted Homily, almost as though she were quoting.

"Famine . . ." said Pod.

Chapter Five

Next morning, when Hendreary heard the news, a conference was called around the doorplate. They all filed in, nervous and grave, and places were allotted them by Lupy. Arrietty was questioned again.

"Are you sure of your dates, Arrietty?"

Yes, Arrietty was sure.

"And of your facts?" Quite sure. Young Tom and his grandfather would leave in three days' time in a gig drawn by a gray pony called Duchess and driven by Tom's uncle, the ostler, whose name was Fred Tarabody and who lived in Leighton Buzzard and worked at the Swan Hotel— what was an ostler she wondered again—and young Tom was worried because he had lost his ferret although it had a bell round its neck and a collar with his name on. He had lost it two days ago down a rabbit hole and was afraid he might have to leave without it, and even if he found it, he wasn't sure they would let him take it with him.

"That's neither there nor here," said Hendreary, drumming his fingers on the table.

They all seemed very anxious and at the same time curiously calm.

Hendreary glanced round the table. "One, two, three, four, five, six, seven, eight, nine," he said gloomily and began to stroke his beard.

"Pod, here," said Homily, "can help borrow."

"And I could, too," put in Arrietty.

"And I could," echoed Timmus in a sudden squeaky voice. They all turned round to look at him, except Hendreary, and Lupy stroked his hair.

"Borrow *what?*" asked Hendreary. "No, it isn't borrowers we want; on the contrary"—he glanced across the table, and Homily, meeting his eye, suddenly turned pink—"it's something left to borrow. They won't leave a crumb behind, those two, not if I know 'em. We'll have to live, from now on, on just what we've saved. . . ."

"For as long as it lasts," said Lupy grimly.

"For as long as it lasts," repeated Hendreary, "and such as it is." All their eyes grew wider.

"Which it won't do forever," said Lupy. She glanced up at her store shelves and quickly away again. She too had become rather red.

"About borrowing . . ." ventured Homily. "I was meaning out-of-doors . . . the vegetable patch . . . beans and peas . . . and suchlike."

"The birds will have them," said Hendreary, "with this house closed and the human beings gone. The birds always know in a trice. . . . And what's more," he went on, "there's more wild things and vermin in these woods than in all the rest of the county put together . . . weasels, stoats, foxes, badgers, shrikes, magpies, sparrow hawks, crows. . . ."

"That's enough, Hendreary," Pod put in quickly. "Homily's feeling faint. . . ."

"It's all right . . ." murmured Homily. She took a sip of water out of the acorn cup, and staring down at the table, she rested her head on her hand.

Hendreary, carried away by the length of his list, seemed not to notice. ". . . owls and buzzards," he concluded in a satisfied voice. "You've seen the skins for yourselves nailed up on the outhouse door, and the birds strung up on a thornbush, gamekeeper's gibbet they call it. He keeps them down all right, when he's well and about. And the boy, too, takes a hand. But with them two gone—!" Hendreary raised his gaunt arms and cast his eyes toward the ceiling.

No one spoke. Arrietty stoke a look at Timmus, whose face had become very pale.

"And when the house is closed and shuttered," Hendreary went on again suddenly, "how do you propose to get out?" He looked round the table triumphantly as one who had made a point. Homily, her head on her hand, was silent. She had begun to regret having spoken.

"There's always ways," murmured Pod.

Hendreary pounced on him. "Such as?" When Pod did not reply at once, Hendreary thundered on, "The last

time they went away we had a plague of field mice . . .
the whole house awash with them, upstairs and down.
Now when they lock up, they lock up proper. Not so
much as a spider could get in!"

"Nor out," said Lupy, nodding.

"Nor out," agreed Hendreary, and as though exhausted
by his own eloquence, he took a sip from the cup.

For a moment or two no one spoke. Then Pod cleared
his throat. "They won't be gone forever," he said.

Hendreary shrugged his shoulders. "Who knows?"

"Looks to me," said Pod, "that they'll always need a

gamekeeper. Say this one goes, another moves in like. Won't be empty long—a good house like this on the edge of the coverts, with water laid on in the washhouse. . . ."

"Who knows?" said Hendreary again.

"Your problem, as I see it," went on Pod, "is to hold out over a period."

"That's it," agreed Hendreary.

"But you don't know for how long; that's your problem."

"That's it," agreed Hendreary.

"The farther you can stretch your food," Pod elaborated, "the longer you'll be able to wait. . . ."

"Stands to reason," said Lupy.

"And," Pod went on, "the fewer mouths you have to feed, the farther the food will stretch."

"That's right," agreed Hendreary.

"Now," went on Pod, "say there are six of you . . ."

"Nine," said Hendreary, looking round the table, "to be exact."

"You don't count us," said Pod. "Homily, Arrietty, and me—we're moving out." There was a stunned silence round the table as Pod, very calm, turned to Homily. "That's right, isn't it?" he asked her.

Homily stared back at him as though he were crazy, and, in despair, he nudged her with his foot. At that she swallowed hastily and began to nod her head. "That's right . . ." she managed to stammer, blinking her eyelids.

Then pandemonium broke out: questions, suggestions, protestations, and arguments. . . . "You don't know what you're saying, Pod," Hendreary kept repeating, and Lupy kept on asking, "Moving out where to?"

"No good being hasty, Pod," Hendreary said at last. "The choice of course is yours. But we're all in this together, and for as long as it lasts"—he glanced around the table as though putting the words on record—"and such as it is, what is ours is yours."

"That's very kind of you, Hendreary," said Pod.

"Not at all," said Hendreary, speaking rather too smoothly, "it stands to reason."

"It's only human," put in Lupy: she was very fond of this word.

"But," went on Hendreary, as Pod remained silent, "I see you've made up your mind."

"That's right," said Pod.

"In which case," said Hendreary, "there's nothing we can do but adjourn the meeting and wish you all good luck!"

"That's right," said Pod.

"Good luck, Pod," said Hendreary.

"Thanks, Hendreary," said Pod.

"And to all three valiant souls—Pod, Homily, and little Arrietty—good luck and good borrowing!"

Homily murmured something and then there was silence: an awkward silence while eyes avoided eyes. "Come on, me old girl," said Pod at last, and turning to Homily, he helped her to her feet. "If you'll excuse us," he said to Lupy, who had become rather red in the face again, "we got one or two plans to discuss."

They all rose, and Hendreary, looking worried, followed Pod to the door. "When do you think of leaving, Pod?"

"In a day or two's time," said Pod, "when the coast's clear down below."

"No hurry, you know," said Hendreary. "And any tackle you want—"

"Thanks," said Pod.

". . . just say the word."

"I will," said Pod. He gave a half-smile, rather shy, and went on through the door.

Chapter Six

Homily went up the laths without speaking; she went straight to the inner room and sat down on the bed. She sat there shivering slightly and staring at her hands.

"I had to say it," said Pod, "and we have to do it, what's more."

Homily nodded.

"You see how we're placed?" said Pod.

Homily nodded again.

"Any suggestions?" said Pod. "Anything else we could do?"

"No," said Homily, "we've got to go. And what's more," she added, "we'd have had to anyway."

"How do you make that out?" said Pod.

"I wouldn't stay here with Lupy," declared Homily, "not if she bribed me with molten gold, which she isn't likely to. I kept quiet, Pod, for the child's sake. A bit of young company, I thought, and a family background. I even kept quiet about the furniture. . . ."

"Yes, you did," said Pod.

"It's only—" said Homily, and again she began to shiver, "that he went on so about the vermin. . . ."

"Yes, he did go on," said Pod.

"Better a place of our own," said Homily.

"Yes," agreed Pod, "better a place of our own. . . ." But he gazed round the room in a hunted kind of way, and his flat round face looked blank.

When Arrietty arrived upstairs with Timmus, she looked both scared and elated.

"Oh," said Homily, "here you are." And she stared rather blankly at Timmus.

"He would come," Arrietty told her, holding him tight by the hand.

"Well, take him along to your room. And tell him a story or something. . . ."

"All right. I will in a minute. But, first, I just wanted to ask you—"

"Later," said Pod, "there'll be plenty of time: we'll talk about everything later."

"That's right," said Homily. "You tell Timmus a story."

"Not about owls?" pleaded Timmus; he still looked rather wide-eyed.

"No," agreed Homily, "not about owls. You ask her to tell you about the dollhouse"—she glanced at Arrietty —"or that other place—what's it called now?—that place with the plaster borrowers?"

But Arrietty seemed not to be listening. "You did mean it, didn't you?" she burst out suddenly.

Homily and Pod stared back at her, startled by her tone. "Of course, we meant it," said Pod.

"Oh," cried Arrietty, "thank goodness . . . thank goodness," and her eyes filled suddenly with tears. "To be out of doors again . . . to see the sun, to . . ." Running forward, she embraced them each in turn. "It will be all right—I know it will!" Aglow with relief and joy, she turned back to Timmus. "Come, Timmus, I know a lovely story—better than the dollhouse—about a whole town of houses: a place called Little Fordham. . . ."

This place, of recent years, had become a kind of legend to borrowers. How they got to know it no one could remember—perhaps a conversation overheard in some kitchen and corroborated later through dining room or nursery—but know of it they did. Little Fordham, it appeared, was a complete model village. Solidly built, it stood out of doors in all weather in the garden of the man who had designed it, and it covered half an acre. It had a church, with organ music laid on, a school, a row of shops, and—because it lay by a stream—its own port, shipping and custom houses. It was inhabited—or so they had heard —by a race of plaster figures, borrower-size, who stood about in frozen positions, or who, wooden-faced and hopeless, traveled interminably in trains. They also knew that from early morning until dusk troops of human beings wound around and about it, removed on asphalt paths and safely enclosed by chains. They knew—as the birds knew—that these human beings would drop litter —sandwich crusts, nuts, buns, half-eaten apples, ("Not that you can live on that sort of stuff," Homily would remark. "I mean, you'd want a change. . . .") But what fascinated them most about the place was the number of empty houses—houses to suit every taste and every size of family: detached, semidetached, stuck together in a row, or standing comfortably each in its separate garden —houses that were solidly built and solidly roofed, set firmly in the ground, and that no human being, however curious, could carelessly wrench open—as they could with dollhouses—and poke about inside. In fact, as Arrietty had heard, doors and windows were one with the structure—there were no kinds of openings at all. But this was a drawback easily remedied. "Not that they'd open up the front doors—" she explained in whispers to Timmus as they lay curled up on Arrietty's bed. "Borrowers wouldn't be so silly: they'd burrow through the soft earth and get in underneath . . . and no human being would know they were there."

"Go on about the trains," whispered Timmus.

And Arrietty went on, and on—explaining and inventing, creating another kind of life. Deep in this world she forgot the present crisis, her parents' worries and her un-

cle's fears, she forgot the dusty drabness of the rooms between the laths, the hidden dangers of the woods outside
and that already she was feeling rather hungry.

Chapter Seven

"But where are we going to?" asked Homily for about the twentieth time. It was two days later, and they were up in Arrietty's room sorting things for the journey, discarding and selecting from oddments spread round on the floor. They could only take—Pod had been very firm about this—what Lupy described as hand luggage. She had given them for this purpose the rubberized sleeve of the waterproof raincoat, which they had neatly cut up into squares.

"I thought," said Pod, "we'd try first to make for that hole in the bank. . . ."

"I don't think I'd relish that hole in the bank," said Homily. "Not without the boot."

"Now, Homily, we've got to go somewhere . . . and it's getting on for spring."

Homily turned and looked at him. "Do you know the way?"

"No," said Pod and went on folding the length of tarred string. "We've got to ask."

"What's the weather like now?" asked Homily.

"That's one of the things," said Pod, "I've told Arrietty to find out."

With some misgivings, but in a spirit of "needs must," they had sent her down the matchstick ladder to interview young Tom. "You've got to ask him to leave us some loophole," Pod had instructed her, "no matter how small, so long as we can get out of doors. If need be, we can undo the luggage and pass the pieces through one by one. If the worst came to the worst, I wouldn't say no to a ground-floor window and something below to break the drop. But like as not, they'll latch those tight and shutter them across. And tell him to leave the wood box well pulled out from the skirting. None of us can move it, not even when it's empty. A nice pickle we'd be in, and all the Hendrearys too, if he trundles off to Leighton Buzzard and leaves us shut in the wall. And tell him where we're making for—that field called Perkin's Beck—but don't tell him nothing about the hole in the bank—and get him to give you a few landmarks, something to put us on our way. It's been a bit chilly indoors lately, for March: ask him if there's snow. If there's snow, we're done: we've got to wait. . . ."

But could they wait, he wondered now as he hung the coil of tarred string on a nail in the lath and thoughtfully took up his hatpin. Hendreary had said in a burst of generosity, "We're all in this together." But Lupy had remarked afterwards, discussing their departure with Homily, "I don't want to seem hard, Homily, but in times like these, it's each one for his own. And in our place you'd say the same." She had been very kind about giving them things —the mackintosh sleeve was a case in point—but the store shelves, they noticed, were suddenly bare: all the food had been whisked away and hidden out of sight, and Lupy had doled out fifteen dried peas that she had said she hoped would "last them." These they kept upstairs, soaking in the soap dish, and Homily would take them down three at a time to boil them on Lupy's stove.

To "last them" for how long, Pod wondered now, as he rubbed a speck of rust off his hatpin. Good as new, he thought, as he tested the point, pure steel and longer than he was. No, they would have to get off, he realized, the minute the coast was clear, snow or no snow. . . .

"Here's someone now," exclaimed Homily. "It must be Arrietty." They went to the hole and helped her onto the floor. The child looked pleased, they noticed, and flushed with the heat of the fire. In one hand she carried a long steel nail, in the other a sliver of cheese. "We can eat this now," she said excitedly. "There's a lot more downstairs: he pushed it through the hole behind the log box. There's a slice of dry bread, some more cheese, six roasted chestnuts, and an egg."

"Not a hen's egg?" said Pod.

"Yes."

"Oh, my," exclaimed Homily, "how are we going to get it up the laths?"

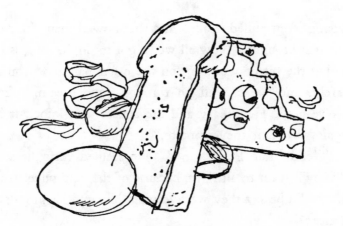

"And how are we going to cook it?" asked Pod.

Homily tossed her head. "I'll boil it with the peas on Lupy's stove. It's our egg; no one can say a word."

"It's boiled already," Arrietty told them, "hard boiled."

"Thank goodness for that," exclaimed Pod. "I'll take down the razor blade—we can bring it up in slices. What's the news?" he asked Arrietty.

"Well, the weather's not bad at all," she said. "Spring-like, he says, when the sun's out, and pretty warm."

"Never mind that," said Pod. "What about the loophole?"

"That's all right too. There's a worn-out place at the bottom of the door—the front door—where feet have been kicking it open, like Tom does when his arms are full of sticks. It's shaped like an arch. But they've nailed a piece of wood across it now to keep the field mice out. Two nails it's got, one on either side. This is one of them;

71

young Tom pulled it out," and she showed them the nail she had brought. "Now all we've got to do, he says, is to swing the bit of wood up on the other nail and prop it safely, and we can all go through—underneath. After we've gone, Hendreary and the cousins can knock it in again, that is if they want to."

"Good," said Pod. "Good." He seemed very pleased. "They'll want to all right, because of the field mice. And when did he say they were leaving, him and his grandpa, I mean?"

"What he said before: the day after tomorrow. But he hasn't found his ferret."

"Good," said Pod again. He wasn't interested in ferrets. "And now we'd better nip down quick and get that food up the laths, or someone might see it first."

Homily and Arrietty climbed down with him to lend a hand. They brought up the bread and cheese and the roasted chestnuts, but the egg they decided to leave. "There's a lot of good food in a hen's egg," Pod pointed out, "and it's all wrapped up already, as you might say, clean and neat in its shell. We'll take that egg along with us and we'll take it just as it is." So, they rolled the egg along inside the wainscot to a shadowy corner in which they had seen shavings. "It can wait for us there," said Pod.

Chapter Eight

On the day the human beings moved out, the borrowers kept very quiet. Sitting round the doorplate table, they listened to the bangings, the bumpings, the runnings up and downstairs with interest and anxiety. They heard voices they had not heard before and sounds that they could not put a name to. They went on keeping quiet . . . long after the final bang of the front door had echoed into silence.

"You never know," Hendreary whispered to Pod. "They might come back for something." But after a while the emptiness of the house below seemed to steal in upon them, seeping mysteriously through the lath and plaster—and it seemed to Pod a final kind of emptiness. "I think it's all right now," he ventured at last. "Suppose one of us went down to reconnoitre?"

"I'll go," said Hendreary, rising to his feet. "None of you move until I give the word. I want the air clear for sound. . . ."

They sat in silence while he was gone. Homily stared

at their three modest bundles lying by the door, strapped by Pod to his hatpin. Lupy had lent Homily a little moleskin jacket—for which Lupy had grown too stout. Arrietty wore a scarf of Eggletina's; the tall, willowy creature had placed it round her neck, wound it three times about, but had said not a word. "Doesn't she ever speak?" Homily had asked once, on a day when she and Lupy had been more friendly. "Hardly ever," Lupy had admitted, "and never smiles. She's been like that for years, ever since that time when as a child she ran away from home. . . ."

After a while Hendreary returned and confirmed that the coast was clear. "But better light your dips; it's later than I thought. . . ."

One after another they scrambled down the matchstick ladder, careless now of noise. The wood box had been pulled well back from the hole, and they flowed out into the room—cathedral-high, it seemed to them, vast and still and echoing, but suddenly all their own. They could do anything, go anywhere. The main window was shuttered as Pod had foreseen, but a smaller, cell-like window, sunk low and deep in the wall, let in a last pale reflection of the sunset. The younger cousins and Arrietty went quite wild, running in and out of the shadows among the chair legs, exploring the cavern below the table top, the underside of which, cobweb hung, danced in the light of their dips. Discoveries were made and treasures found —under rugs, down cracks in the floor, between loose hearth stones—here a pin, there a matchstick, a button, an

74

old collar-stud, a blackened farthing, a coral bead, a hook without its eye, and a broken piece of lead from a lead pencil. (Arrietty pounced on this last and pushed it into her pocket; she had had to leave her diary behind, with other nonessentials, but one never knew. . . .) Then dips were set down and everybody started climbing—except Lupy, who was too stout; and Pod and Homily who watched silently, standing beside the door. Hendreary tried an overcoat on a nail for the sake of what he might find in the pockets, but he had not Pod's gift for climbing fabric and had to be rescued by one of his sons from where he hung, perspiring and breathing hard, clinging to a sleeve button.

"He should have gone up by the front buttonholes," Pod whispered to Homily. "You can get your toes in and pull the pocket toward you like by folding in the stuff. You never want to make direct for a pocket. . . ."

"I wish," Homily whispered back, "they'd stop this until we're gone." It was the kind of occasion she would have enjoyed in an ordinary way—a glorious bargain hunt—findings keepings with no holds barred; but the shadow of their ordeal hung over her and made such antics seem foolish.

"Now," exclaimed Hendreary suddenly, straightening his clothes and coming toward them as though he had guessed her thought, "we'd better test out this escape route."

He called up his two elder sons, and together the three

75

of them, after spitting on their hands, laid hold of the piece of wood that covered the hole in the door.

"One, two, three—hup!" intoned Hendreary, ending on a grunt. They gave a mighty heave and the slab of wood pivoted slowly, squeaking on its one nail, revealing the arch below.

Pod took his dip and peered through. Grass and stones he saw for a moment and some kind of shadowy movement before a draft caught the flame and nearly blew it out. He sheltered the flame with his hand and tried again.

"Quick, Pod," gasped Hendreary, "this wood's heavy. . . ."

Pod peered through again. No grass now, no stones—a rippling blackness, the faintest snuffle of breath, and

two sudden pin points of fire, unblinking and deadly still.

"Drop the wood," breathed Pod—he spoke without moving his lips. "Quick," he added under his breath as Hendreary seemed to hesitate, "can't you hear the bell?" And he stood there as though frozen, holding his dip steadily before him.

Down came the wood with a clap, and Homily screamed. "You saw it?" said Pod, turning. He set down his dip and wiped his brow on his sleeve; he was breathing rather heavily.

"Saw it?" cried Homily. "In another second it would have been in here amongst us."

Timmus began to cry and Arrietty ran to him. "It's all right, Timmus, it's gone now. It was only an old ferret, an old tame ferret. Come, I'll tell you a story." She took him under a rough wooden desk where she had seen an old account book; setting it up on its outer leaves, she made it into a tent. They crept inside, just the two of them, and between the sheltering pages they soon felt very cozy.

"Whatever was it?" cried Lupy, who had missed the whole occurrence.

"Like she said—a ferret," announced Pod. "That boy's ferret I shouldn't wonder. If so, it'll be all round the house from now on seeking a way to get in. . . ." He turned to Homily. "There'll be no leaving here tonight."

Lupy, standing in the hearth where the ashes were still warm, sat down suddenly on an empty matchbox that gave an ominous crack. ". . . nearly in amongst us," she repeated faintly, closing her eyes against the ghastly vision. A faint cloud of wood ash rose slowly around her, which she fanned away with her hand.

"Well, Pod," said Hendreary after a pause, "that's that."

"How do you mean?" said Pod.

"You can't go that way. That ferret'll be round the house for weeks. . . ."

"Yes . . ." said Pod, and was silent a moment. "We'll have to think again." He gazed in a worried way at the shuttered window; the smaller one was a wall aperture, glazed to give light but with the glass built in—no possibility there.

"Let's have a look at the washhouse," he said. This door luckily had been left ajar, and, dip in hand, he slid through the crack. Hendreary and Homily slid through after him, and after a while Arrietty followed. Filled with curiosity, she longed to see the washhouse, as she longed to see every corner of this vast human edifice now that they had it to themselves. The chimney she saw, in the flickering light of the dip, stood back to back with the one in the living room; in it there stood a dingy cooking stove. Flagstones covered the floor. An old mangle stood in one corner, in the other a copper for boiling clothes. Against the wall, below the window, towered a stone sink. The window above the sink was heavily shuttered and rather high. The door, which led outside, was bolted in two places and had a zinc panel across the bottom, reinforcing the wood.

"Nothing doing here," said Hendreary.

"No," agreed Pod.

They went back to the living room. Lupy had recovered somewhat and had risen from the matchbox, leaving it slightly askew. She had brushed herself down and was packing up the borrowings preparatory to going upstairs. "Come along, chicks," she called to her children. "It's nearly midnight and we'll have all day tomorrow. . . ." When she saw Hendreary, she said, "I thought we might go up now and have a bite of supper." She gave a little laugh. "I'm a wee bit tired—what with ferrets and so on and so forth."

Hendreary looked at Pod. "What about you?" he said, and as Pod hesitated, Hendreary turned to Lupy. "They've had a hard day too—what with ferrets and so on and so forth—and they can't leave here tonight. . . ."

"Oh?" said Lupy, and stared. She seemed slightly taken aback.

"What have we got for supper?" Hendreary asked her.

"Six boiled chestnuts"—she hesitated—"and a smoked minnow each for you and the boys."

"Well, perhaps we could open something," suggested Hendreary after a moment. Again Lupy hesitated, and the pause became too long. "Why, of course—" she began in a flustered voice, but Homily interrupted.

"Thank you very much. It's very kind of you, but

we've got three roast chestnuts ourselves . . . and an egg."

"An egg," echoed Lupy, amazed. "What kind of an egg?"

"A hen's egg . . ."

"A *hen's* egg," echoed Lupy again, as though a hen were a pterodactyl or a fabulous bird like the phoenix. "Wherever did you get it?"

"Oh," said Homily, "it's just an egg we had."

"And we'd like to stay down here a bit," put in Pod, "if that's all right with you."

"Quite all right," said Lupy stiffly. She still looked amazed about the egg. "Come, Timmus."

It took some minutes to round them all up. There was a lot of running back for things, chatter at the foot of the ladder, callings, scoldings, giggles, and "take-cares." "One at a time," Lupy kept saying, "one at a time, my lambs." But at last they were all up and their voices became more muffled as they left the echoing landing for the inner rooms beyond. Light running sounds were heard, small rollings, and the faintest of distant squeakings.

"How like mice we must sound to humans," Arrietty realized as she listened from below. But after a while even these small patterings ceased and all became quiet and still. Arrietty turned and looked at her parents: at last they were alone.

Chapter Nine

"Between the devil and the deep blue sea, that's us," said Pod with a wan smile. He was quoting from Arrietty's diary and proverb book.

They sat grouped on the hearth where the stones were warm. The iron shovel, still too hot to sit on, lay sprawled across the ashes. Homily had pulled up the crushed matchbox lid on which, with her lighter weight, she could sit comfortably. Pod and Arrietty perched on a charred stick; the three lighted dips were set between them on the ash. Shadows lay about them in the vast confines of the room, and now that the Hendrearys were out of earshot (sitting down to supper most likely), they felt drowned in the spreading silence.

After a while this was broken by the faint tinkle of a bell—quite close it seemed suddenly. There was a slight scratching sound and the lightest, most delicate of snuffles. They all glanced wide-eyed at the door, which, from where they sat, was deeply sunk in shadow.

"It can't get in, can it?" whispered Homily.

"Not a hope," said Pod. "Let it scratch . . . we're all right here."

All the same Arrietty threw a searching glance up the wide chimney; the stones, she thought, if the worst came to the worst, looked uneven enough to climb. Then suddenly, far, far above her, she saw a square of violet sky and in it a single star, and, for some reason, felt reassured.

"As I see it," said Pod, "we can't go and we can't stay."

"And that's how I see it," said Homily.

"Suppose," suggested Arrietty, "we climbed up the chimney onto the thatch?"

"And then what?" said Pod.

"I don't know," said Arrietty.

"There we'd be," said Pod.

"Yes, there we'd be," agreed Homily unhappily, "even supposing we could climb a chimney, which I doubt."

There was a few moments' silence, then Pod said solemnly, "Homily, there's nothing else for it . . ."

". . . but what?" asked Homily, raising a startled face. Lit from below, it looked curiously bony and was streaked here and there with ash. And Arrietty, who guessed what was coming, gripped her two hands beneath her knees and stared fixedly down at the shovel, which lay sideways across the hearth.

"But to bury our pride, that's what," said Pod.

"How do you mean?" asked Homily weakly, but she knew quite well what he meant.

"We got to go, quite open-like, to Lupy and Hendreary and ask them to let us stay. . . ."

Homily put her thin hands on either side of her thin face and stared at him dumbly.

"For the child's sake . . ." Pod pointed out gently.

The tragic eyes swiveled round to Arrietty and back again.

"A few dried peas, that's all we'd ask for," went on Pod very gently, "just water to drink and a few dried peas. . . ."

Still Homily did not speak.

"And we'd say they could keep the furniture in trust like," suggested Pod.

Homily stirred at last. "They'd keep the furniture anyway," she said huskily.

"Well, what about it?" asked Pod after a moment, watching her face.

Homily looked round the room in a hunted kind of way, up at the chimney then down at the ashes at their feet. At last she nodded her head. "Should we go up now," she suggested after a moment in a dispirited kind of voice, "while they're all at supper and get it over with?"

"Might as well," said Pod. He stood up and put out a hand to Homily. "Come on, me old girl," he coaxed her. Homily rose slowly and Pod turned to Arrietty, Homily's hand pulled under his arm. Standing beside his wife, he drew himself up to his full six inches. "There's two kinds of courage I know of," he said, "and your mother's got both of 'em; you make a note of that, my girl, when you're writing in your diary. . . ."

But Arrietty was gazing past him into the room; she was staring white-faced into the shadows beyond the log box toward the scullery door.

"Something moved," she whispered.

Pod turned, following the direction of her eyes. "What like?" he asked sharply.

"Something furry . . ."

They all froze. Then Homily, with a cry, ran out from between them. Amazed and aghast, they watched her scramble off the hearth and run with outstretched arms toward the shadows beyond the log box. She seemed to be laughing—or crying—her breath coming in little gasps. ". . . the dear boy, the good boy . . . the blessed creature!"

"It's Spiller!" cried Arrietty on a shout of joy.

She ran forward too, and they dragged him out of the shadows, pulled him onto the hearth and beside the dips, where the light shone warmly on his suit of moleskins, worn now, slightly tattered, and shorter in the leg. His feet were bare and gleaming with black mud. He seemed to have grown heavier and taller. His hair was still as ragged and his pointed face as brown. They did not think to ask him where he had come from; it was enough that he was there. Spiller, it seemed to Arrietty, always materialized out of air and dissolved again as swiftly.

"Oh, Spiller!" gasped Homily, who was not supposed

to like him. "In the nick of time, the very nick of time!" And she sat down on the charred stick, which flew up, the farther end scattering a cloud of ash, and burst into happy tears.

"Nice to see you, Spiller," said Pod, smiling and looking him up and down. "Come for your summer clothes?" Spiller nodded; bright-eyed, he gazed about the room, taking in the bundles strapped to the hatpin, the pulled-out position of the log box, the odd barenesses and rearrangements that signify human departure. But he made no comment. Countrymen, such as Spiller and Pod were, do not rush into explanations; faced with whatever strange evidence, they mind their manners and bide their time. "Well, I happen to know they're not ready," Pod went on. "She's sewn the vest, mind, but she hasn't joined up the trousers. . . ."

Spiller nodded again. His eyes sought out Arrietty who, ashamed of her first outburst, had become suddenly shy and had withdrawn behind the shovel.

"Well," said Pod at last, looking about as though aware suddenly of strangeness in their surroundings, "you find us in a nice sort of pickle. . . ."

"Moving house?" asked Spiller casually.

"In a manner of speaking," said Pod. And as Homily dried her eyes on her apron and began to pin up her hair, he outlined the story to Spiller in a few rather fumbling words. Spiller listened with one eyebrow raised and his mocking v-shaped mouth twisted up at the corners. This was Spiller's famous expression, Arrietty remembered, no matter what you were telling him.

". . . and so," said Pod, shrugging his shoulders, "you see how we're placed?"

Spiller nodded, looking thoughtful.

"Must be pretty hungry now, that ferret," Pod went on, "poor creature. Can't hunt with a bell: the rabbits hear him coming. Gone in a flash the rabbits are. But with our short legs he'd be on us in a trice—bell or no bell. But how did you manage?" Pod asked suddenly.

"The usual," said Spiller.

"What usual?"

Spiller jerked his head toward the washhouse. "The drain, of course," he said.

Chapter Ten

"What drain?" asked Homily, staring.

"The one in the floor," said Spiller, as though she ought to have known. "The sink's no good—got an 's' bend. And they keep the lid on the copper."

"I didn't see any drain in the floor . . ." said Pod.

"It's under the mangle," explained Spiller.

"But—" went on Homily. "I mean, do you always come by the drain?"

"And go," said Spiller.

"Undercover, like," Pod pointed out to Homily. "Doesn't have to bother with the weather."

"Or the woods," said Homily.

"That's right," agreed Spiller. "You don't want to bother with the woods. Not the woods," he repeated thoughtfully.

"Where does the drain come out?" asked Pod.

"Down by the kettle," said Spiller.

"What kettle?"

"His kettle," put in Arrietty excitedly. "That kettle he's got by the stream. . . ."

"That's right," said Spiller.

Pod looked thoughtful. "Do the Hendrearys know this?"

Spiller shook his head. "Never thought to tell them," he said.

Pod was silent a moment and then he said, "Could anyone use this drain?"

"No reason why not," said Spiller. "Where you making for?"

"We don't know yet," said Pod.

Spiller frowned and scratched his knee where the black mud, drying in the warmth of the ash, had turned to a powdery gray. "Ever thought of the town?" he asked.

"Leighton Buzzard?"

"No," exclaimed Spiller scornfully. "Little Fordham."

Had Spiller suggested a trip to the moon, they could not have looked more astonished. Homily's face was a study in disbelief, as though she thought Spiller was romancing. Arrietty became very still; she seemed to be holding her breath. Pod looked ponderously startled.

"So there is such a place?" he said slowly.

"Of course there is such a place," snapped Homily. "Everyone knows that; what they don't know exactly is —where? And I doubt if Spiller does either. . . ."

"Two days down the river," said Spiller, "if the stream's running good."

"Oh," said Pod.

"You mean we have to swim for it?" snapped Homily.

"I got a boat," said Spiller.

"Oh, my goodness . . ." murmured Homily, suddenly deflated.

"Big?" asked Pod.

"Fair," said Spiller.

"Could she take passengers?" asked Pod.

"Could do," said Spiller.

"Oh, my goodness . . ." murmured Homily again.

"What's the matter, Homily?" asked Pod.

"Can't see myself in a boat," said Homily. "Not on the water, I can't."

"Well, a boat's not much good on dry land," said Pod. "To get something, you got to risk something—that's how it goes. We got to find somewhere to live."

"There might be something, say, in walking distance," faltered Homily.

"Such as?"

"Well," said Homily unhappily, throwing a quick glance at Spiller, "say, for instance . . . Spiller's kettle."

"Not much accommodation in a kettle," said Pod.

"More than there was in a boot," retorted Homily.

"Now, Homily," said Pod, suddenly firm, "you wouldn't be happy, not for twenty-four hours, in a kettle; and inside a week you'd be on at me night and day to find some kind of craft to get you downstream to Little Fordham. Here you are with the chance of a good home, fresh start, and a free passage, and all you do is go on like a maniac about a drop of clean running water. Now, if it was the drain you objected to—"

Homily turned to Spiller. "What sort of boat?" she asked nervously. "I mean, if I could picture it like . . ."

Spiller thought a moment. "Well," he said, "it's wooden."

"Yes?" said Homily.

Spiller tried again. "Well, it's like . . . you might say it was something like a knife box."

"How much like?" asked Pod.

"Very like," said Spiller.

"In fact," declared Homily triumphantly, "it *is* a knife box?"

Spiller nodded. "That's right," he admitted.

"Flat-bottomed?" asked Pod.

"With divisions, like, for spoons, forks, and so on?" put in Homily.

"That's right," agreed Spiller, replying to both.

"Tarred and waxed at the seams?"

"Waxed," said Spiller.

"Sounds all right to me," said Pod. "What do you say, Homily?" It sounded better to her too, Pod realized, but he saw she was not quite ready to commit herself. He turned again to Spiller. "What do you do for power?"

"Power?"

"Got some kind of sail?"

Spiller shook his head. "Take her downstream, loaded —with a paddle; pole her back upstream in ballast. . . ."

"I see," said Pod. He sounded rather impressed. "You go often to Little Fordham?"

"Pretty regular," said Spiller.

"I see," said Pod again. "Sure you could give us a lift?"

"Call back for you," said Spiller, "at the kettle, say. Got to go upstream to load."

"Load what?" asked Homily bluntly.

"The boat," said Spiller.

"I know that," said Homily, "but with what?"

"Now, Homily," put in Pod, "that's Spiller's business. No concern of ours. Does a bit of trading up and down the river I shouldn't wonder. Mixed cargo, eh, Spiller? Nuts, birds' eggs, meat, minnows . . . that sort of tackle —more or less what he brings Lupy."

"Depends what they're short of," said Spiller.

"They?" exclaimed Homily.

"Now, Homily," Pod admonished her, "Spiller's got his customers. Stands to reason. We're not the only borrowers in the world, remember. Not by a long chalk. . . ."

"But these ones at Little Fordham," Homily pointed out, "they say they're made of plaster?"

"That's right," said Spiller, "painted over. All of a piece . . . except one," he added.

"One live one?" asked Pod.

"That's right," said Spiller.

"Oh, I wouldn't like that," exclaimed Homily, "I wouldn't like that at all: not to be the one live borrower

93

among a lot of dummy waxworks or whatever they call themselves. Get on my nerves that would. . . ."

"They don't bother him," said Spiller. "Leastways not as much, he says, as a whole lot of live ones might."

"Well, that's a nice friendly attitude, I must say," snapped Homily. "Nice kind of welcome we'll get, I can see, when we turn up there unexpected. . . ."

"Plenty of houses," said Spiller, "no sort of need to live close. . . ."

"And he doesn't own the places," Pod reminded her.

"That's true," said Homily.

"What about it, Homily?" said Pod.

"I don't mind," said Homily, "providing we live near the shops . . ."

"There's nothing in the shops," explained Pod in a patient voice, "or so I've heard tell, but bananas and suchlike made of plaster and all stuck down in a lump."

"No, but it sounds nice," said Homily. "Say you were talking to Lupy—"

"But you won't be talking to Lupy," said Pod. "Lupy won't even know we're gone until she wakes up tomorrow morning thinking that she's got to get us breakfast. No, Homily," he went on earnestly, "you don't want to make for shopping centers and all that sort of caper; better some quiet little place down by the water's edge. You won't want to be everlastingly carting water. And, say Spiller comes down pretty regular with a nice bit of cargo, you want somewhere he can tie up and unload. . . . Plenty of time, once we get there, to have a look round and take our pick."

"Take our pick . . ." Suddenly Homily felt the magic of these words: they began to work inside her—champagne bubbles of excitement welling up and up—until, at last, she flung her hands together in a sudden joyful clap. "Oh Pod," she breathed, her eyes brimming, as, startled by the noise, he turned sharply toward her. "Think of it —all those houses . . . We could try them *all* out if we wanted, one after another. What's to prevent us?"

"Common sense," said Pod; he smiled at Arrietty. "What do you say, lass? Shops or water?"

Arrietty cleared her throat. "Down by water," she whispered huskily, her eyes shining and her face tremulous in the dancing light of the dip, "at least to start with. . . ."

There was a short pause. Pod glanced down at his tackle strapped to the hatpin and up at the clock on the wall. "Getting on for half-past one," he said. "Time we had a look at this drain. What do you say, Spiller? Could you spare us a minute? And show us the ropes like?"

"Oh," exclaimed Homily, dismayed, "I thought Spiller was coming with us."

"Now, Homily," explained Pod, "it's a long trek and he's only just arrived; he won't want to go back right away."

"I don't see why not if his clothes aren't ready—that's what you came for, isn't it, Spiller?"

"That and other things," said Pod. "Daresay he's brought a few oddments for Lupy."

"That's all right," said Spiller. "I can tip 'em out on the floor."

"And you will come?" cried Homily.

Spiller nodded. "Might as well."

Even Pod seemed slightly relieved. "That's very civil of you, Spiller," he said, "very civil indeed." He turned to Arrietty. "Now, Arrietty, take a dip and go and fetch the egg."

"Oh, don't let's bother with the egg," said Homily.

Pod gave her a look. "You go and get that egg, Arrietty. Just roll it along in front of you into the wash-house, but be careful with the light near those shavings. Homily, you bring the other two dips and I'll get the tackle. . . ."

Chapter Eleven

As they filed through the crack of the door onto the stone flags of the washhouse, they heard the ferret again. But Homily now felt brave. "Scratch away," she dared it happily, secure in their prospect of escape. But when they stood at last, grouped beneath the mangle and staring down at the drain, her new-found courage ebbed a little and she murmured, "Oh, my goodness. . . ." Very deep and dark and well-like it seemed, sunk below the level of the floor. The square grating that usually covered it lay beside it at an angle, and in the yawning blackness she could see the reflections of their dips. A dank draft quivered round the candle flames, and there was a sour smell of yellow soap, stale disinfectant, and tea leaves.

"What's that at the bottom?" she asked, peering down. "Water?"

"Slime," said Spiller.

"Jellied soap," put in Pod quickly.

"And we've got to wade through that?"

"It isn't deep," said Spiller.

"Not as though this drain was a sewer," said Pod, trying to sound comforting and hearty. "Beats me though," he went on to Spiller, "how you manage to move this grating."

Spiller showed him. Lowering the dip, he pointed out a short length of what looked like brass curtain rod, strong but hollow, perched on a stone at the bottom of the well and leaning against the side. The top of this rod protruded slightly above the mouth of the drain. The grating, when in place, lay loosely on its worn rim of cement. Spiller explained how, by exerting all his strength on the rod from below, he could raise one corner of the grating—as a washerwoman with a prop can raise up a clothesline. He would then slide the base of the prop onto the raised stone in the base of the shaft, thus holding the contraption in place. Spiller would then swing himself up to the mouth of the drain on a piece of twine tied to a rung of the grating. "Only about twice my height," he explained. The twine, Pod gathered, was a fixture. The double twist round the light iron rung was hardly noticeable from above, and the length of the twine, when not in use, hung downwards into the drain. Should Spiller want to remove the grating entirely, as was the case today, after scrambling through the aperture raised by the rod, he would pull the twine after him, fling it around one of the stays of the mangle above his head, and would drag and pull on the end. Sometimes, Spiller explained, the grating slid easily; at other times it stuck on an angle. In which event, Spiller would produce a small but heavy bolt, kept specially for the purpose, which he would wind into the free end of his halyard and, climbing into the girder-like structure at the base of the mangle, would swing himself out on the bolt, which, sinking under his weight, exerted a pull on the grating.

"Very ingenious," said Pod. Dip in hand he went deeper under the mangle, examined the wet twine, pulled on the knots, and finally, as though to test its weight, gave the grating a shove. It slid smoothly on the worn flagstones. "Easier to shove than to lift," he remarked. Arrietty, glancing upwards, saw vast shadows on the washhouse ceiling—moving and melting, advancing and receding— in the flickering light from their dips: great wheels, handles, rollers, shifting spokes . . . as though, she thought, the mangle under which they stood was silently and magically turning. . . .

On the ground, beside the drain, she saw an object she recognized: the lid of an aluminum soapbox, the one in which the summer before last Spiller had spun her down the river, and from which he used to fish. It was packed now with some kind of cargo and covered with a piece of worn hide—possibly a rat skin—strapped over lid and all with lengths of knotted twine. From a hole bored in one end of the rim a second piece of twine protruded. "I pull her up by that," explained Spiller, following the direction of her eyes.

"I see how you get up," said Homily unhappily, peering into the slime, "but it's how you get down that worries me."

"Oh, you just drop," said Spiller. He took hold of the twine as he spoke and began to drag the tin lid away toward the door.

"It's all right, Homily," Pod promised hurriedly, "we'll let you down on the bolt," and he turned quickly to Spiller. "Where you going with that?" he asked.

Spiller, it seemed, not wishing to draw attention to the drain, was going to unpack next door. The house being free of humans and the log box pulled out, there was no need to go upstairs. He could dump what he'd brought beside the hole in the skirting.

While he was gone, Pod outlined a method of procedure. ". . . if Spiller agrees," he kept saying, courteously conceding the leadership.

Spiller did agree, or rather he raised no objections. The empty soapbox lid, lightly dangling, was lowered onto the mud; into this they dropped the egg—rolling it to the edge of the drain as though it were a giant rugby football, with a final kick from Pod to send it spinning and keep it clear of the sides. It plopped into the soapbox lid with an ominous crack. This did not matter, however, the egg being hard-boiled.

Homily, with not a few nervous exclamations, was lowered next, seated astride the bolt; with one hand she clung to the twine, in the other she carried a lighted dip. When she climbed off the bolt into the lid of the soapbox, the latter slid swiftly away on the slime, and Homily, for an anxious moment, disappeared along the drain. Spiller drew her back, however, hand over hand. And there she sat behind the egg, grumbling a little, but with her candle still alight. "Two can go in the lid," Spiller had announced, and Arrietty (who secretly had longed to try the drop) was lowered considerably, dip in hand, in the same respectful way. She settled herself opposite her mother with the egg wobbling between them.

"You two are the light-bearers," said Pod. "All you've got to do is to sit quite still and steady the egg—move the lights as we say . . ."

There was a little shuffling about in the lid and some slightly perilous balancing as Homily, who had never liked traveling—as human beings would say—back to the engine, stood up to change seats with Arrietty. "Keep a good hold on that string," she kept imploring Spiller as she completed this maneuver, but soon she and Arrietty were seated again face to face, each with their candle and the egg between their knees. Arrietty was laughing.

"Now I'm going to let you go a little ways," warned Spiller and paid out a few inches of twine. Arrietty and Homily slid smoothly under the roof of their arched tunnel, which gleamed wetly in the candlelight. Arrietty put out a finger and touched the gleaming surface: it seemed to be made of baked clay.

"Don't touch *anything*," hissed Homily, shudderingly, "and don't breathe either—not unless you have to."

Arrietty, lowering her dip, peered over the side at the mud. "There's a fishbone," she remarked, "and a tin bottle top. And a hairpin . . ." she added on a pleased note.

"Don't even *look*," shuddered Homily.

"A hairpin would be useful," Arrietty pointed out.

Homily closed her eyes. "All right," she said, her face drawn with the effort not to mind. "Pick it out quickly and drop it, sharp, in the bottom of the boat. And wipe your hands on my apron."

"We can wash it in the river," Arrietty pointed out.

Homily nodded; she was trying not to breathe.

Over Homily's shoulder Arrietty could see into the well of the drain; a bulky object was coming down the shaft: it was Pod's tackle, waterproof-wrapped and strapped securely to his hatpin. It wobbled on the mud with a slight squelch. Pod, after a while, came after it. Then came Spiller. For a moment the surface seemed to bear their weight then, knee-deep, they sank in slime.

Spiller removed the length of curtain rod from the stone and set it up inconspicuously in the corner of the shaft. Before their descent he and Pod must have placed the grating above more conveniently in position: a deft pull by Spiller on the twine and they heard it clamp down into place—a dull metallic sound that echoed hollowly along the length of their tunnel. Homily gazed into the blackness ahead as though following its flight. "Oh, my goodness," she breathed as the sound died; she felt suddenly shut in.

"Well," announced Pod in a cheerful voice, coming up behind them, and he placed a hand on the rim of their lid, "we're off!"

Chapter Twelve

Spiller they saw, to control them on a shorter length, was rolling up the towline. Not that towline was quite the right expression under the circumstances; the drain ran ahead on a slight downwards incline and Spiller functioned more as a sea anchor and used the twine as a brake.

"Here we go," said Pod, and gave the lid a slight push. They slid ahead on the slippery scum, to be lightly checked by Spiller. The candlelight danced and shivered on the arched roof and about the dripping walls. So thick and soapy was the scum on which they rode that Pod, behind them, seemed more to be leading his bundle than dragging it behind him. Sometimes, even, it seemed to be leading him.

"Whoa, there!" he would cry on such occasions. He was in very good spirits, and had been, Arrietty noticed, from the moment he set foot in the drain. She, too, felt strangely happy. Here they were, the two she held most dear, with Spiller added, making their way toward the dawn. The drain held no fears for Arrietty, leading as it did toward a life to be lived away from dust and candle-light and confining shadows—a life on which the sun would shine by day and the moon by night.

She twisted round in her seat in order to see ahead, and as she did so, a great aperture opened to her left and a dank draft flattened the flame of her candle. She shielded it quickly with her hand and Homily did the same.

"That's where the pipe from the sink comes in," said Spiller, "and the overflow from the copper. . . ."

There were other openings as they went along, drains that branched into darkness and ran away uphill. Where these joined the main drain a curious collection of flot-sam and jetsam piled up over which they had to drag the soap lid. Arrietty and Homily got out for this to make less weight for the men. Spiller knew all these branch drains by name and the exact position of each cottage or house concerned. Arrietty began, at last, to understand the vast resources of Spiller's trading. "Not that you get up into all of 'em," he explained. "I don't mind an 's' bend, but where you get an 's' bend, you're apt to get a brass grille or suchlike in the plug hole."

Once he said, jerking his head toward the mouth of a circular cavern, "Holmcroft, that is. . . . Nothing but bath water from now on. . . ." And, indeed, this cavern, as they slid past it, had looked cleaner than most—a shin-ing cream-colored porcelain—and the air from that point onwards, Arrietty noticed, smelled far less strongly of tea leaves.

Every now and again they came across small branches —of ash or holly—rammed so securely into place that they would have difficulty maneuvering round them. They were set, Arrietty noticed, at almost regular intervals. "I can't think how these tree things get down drains, anyway," Homily exclaimed irritably when, for about the fifth time, the soapbox lid was turned up sideways and eased past and she and Arrietty stood ankle-deep in jetsam, shielding their dips with their hands.

"I put them there," said Spiller, holding the boat for them to get in again. The drain at this point dropped more steeply. As Homily stepped in opposite Arrietty, the soapbox lid suddenly slid away, dragging Spiller after. He slipped and skidded on the surface of the mud, but miraculously he kept his balance. They fetched up in a tangle against the trunk of one of Spiller's treelike erections and Arrietty's dip went overboard. "So that's what they're for," exclaimed Homily as she coaxed her own flattened wick back to brightness to give Arrietty a light.

But Spiller did not answer straight away. He pushed past the obstruction, and as they waited for Pod to catch up, he said suddenly, "Could be . . ."

Pod looked weary when he came up to them. He was panting a little and had stripped off his jacket and slung it round his shoulders. "The last lap's always the longest," he pointed out.

"Would you care for a ride in the lid?" asked Homily. "Do, Pod!"

"No, I'm better walking," said Pod.

"Then give me your jacket," said Homily. She folded it gently across her knees and patted it soberly as though (thought Arrietty, watching) it were tired, like Pod.

And then they were off again—an endless, monotonous vista of circular walls. Arrietty after a while began to doze; she slid forward against the egg, her head caught up on one knee. Just before she fell asleep, she felt Homily slide the dip from her drooping fingers and wrap her round with Pod's coat.

When she awoke, the scene was much the same: shadows sliding and flickering on the wet ceiling, Spiller's narrow face palely lit as he trudged along, and the bulky shape beyond that was Pod. Her mother, across the egg, smiled at her bewilderment. "Forgotten where you were?" asked Homily.

Arrietty nodded. Her mother held a dip in either hand, and the wax, Arrietty noticed, had burned very low. "Must be nearly morning," Arrietty remarked. She still felt very sleepy.

"Shouldn't wonder . . ." said Homily.

The walls slid by, unbroken except for archlike thickenings at regular intervals where one length of pipe joined another. And when they spoke, their voices echoed hollowly back and forth along the tunnel.

"Aren't there any more branch drains?" Arrietty asked after a moment.

Spiller shook his head. "No more now. Holmcroft was the last. . . ."

"But that was ages ago . . . we must be nearly there."

"Getting on," said Spiller.

Arrietty shivered and drew Pod's coat more tightly around her shoulders; the air seemed fresher suddenly and curiously free from smell. "Or perhaps," she thought, "we've grown more used to it. . . ." There was no sound except for the whispering slide of the soapbox lid and the regular plop and suction of Pod's and Spiller's footsteps. But the silt seemed rather thinner: there was an occasional grating sound below the base of the tin lid as though it rode on grit. Spiller stood still. "Listen!" he said.

They were all quiet but could hear nothing except Pod's breathing and a faint musical drip somewhere just ahead of them. "Better push on," said Homily suddenly, break-

ing the tension. "These dips aren't going to last for ever."

"Quiet!" cried Spiller again. Then they heard a faint drumming sound, hardly more than a vibration.

"Whatever is it?" asked Homily.

"Can only be Holmcroft," said Spiller. He stood rigid, with one hand raised, listening intently. "But," he said, turning to Pod, "who ever'd be having a bath at this time o' night?"

Pod shook his head. "It's morning by now," he said, "must be getting on for six."

The drumming sound grew louder, less regular, more like a leaping and a banging. . . .

"We've got to run for it—" cried Spiller. Towline in hand, he swung the tin lid round and, taking the lead, flew ahead into the tunnel. Arrietty and Homily banged and rattled behind him. Dragged on the short line, they swung

shatteringly, thrown from wall to wall. But, panic-stricken at the thought of total darkness, each shielded the flame of her candle. Homily stretched out a free hand to Pod who caught hold of it just as his bundle bore down on him, knocking him over. He fell across it, still gripping Homily's hand, and was carried swiftly along.

"Out and up," cried Spiller from the shadows ahead, and they saw the glistening twigs wedged tautly against the roof. "Let the traps go," he was shouting. "Come on —climb!"

They each seized a branch and swung themselves up and wedged themselves tight against the ceiling. The over-turned dips lay guttering in the tin lid and the air was filled with the sound of galloping water. In the jerking light from the dips they saw the first pearly bubbles and the racing, dancing, silvery bulk behind. And then all was choking, swirling, scented darkness. . . .

After the first few panic-stricken seconds, Arrietty found she could breathe and that the sticks still held. A millrace of hot scented water swilled through her clothes, piling against her at one moment, falling away the next. Sometimes it bounced above her shoulders, drenching her face and hair; at others it swirled steadily about her waist and tugged at her legs and feet. "Hold on," shouted Pod above the turmoil.

"Die down soon," shouted Spiller.

"You there, Arrietty?" gasped Homily. They were all

there and all breathing, and, even as they realized this, the water began to drop in level and run less swiftly. Without the brightness of the dips, the darkness about them seemed less opaque, as though a silvery haze rose from the water itself, which seemed now to be running well below them, and from the sound of it, as innocent and steady as a brook.

After a while they climbed down into it and felt a smoothly running warmth about their ankles. At this level they could see a faint translucence where the surface of the water met the blackness of the walls. "Seems lighter," said Pod wonderingly. He seemed to perceive some shifting in the darkness where Spiller splashed and probed. "Anything there?" he asked.

"Not a thing," said Spiller.

Their baggage had disappeared—egg, soapbox lid and all—swept away on the flood.

"And now what?" asked Pod dismally.

But Spiller seemed quite unworried. "Pick it up later," he said. ". . . nothing to hurt. And saves carting."

Homily was sniffing the air. "Sandalwood!" she exclaimed suddenly to Arrietty. "Your father's favorite soap."

But Arrietty, her hand on a twig to steady herself against the warm flow eddying past her ankles, did not reply; she was staring straight ahead down the incline of the drain. A bead of light hung in the darkness. For a moment she thought that, by some miraculous chance, it might be one of the dips—then she saw it was completely round and curiously steady. And mingled with the scent of sandalwood she smelled another smell—minty, grassy, mildly earthy . . .

"It's dawn," she announced in a wondering voice. "And what's more," she went on, staring spellbound at the distant pearl of light, "that's the end of the drain."

Chapter Thirteen

The warmth from the bath water soon wore off and the rest of the walk was chilly. The circle of light grew larger and brighter as they advanced toward it until, at last, its radiance dazzled their eyes.

"The sun's out," Arrietty decided. It was a pleasant thought, soaked to the skin as they were, and they slightly quickened their steps. The bath-water flow had sunk to the merest trickle and the drain felt gloriously clean.

Arrietty, too, felt somehow purged as though all traces of the old dark, dusty life had been washed away—even from their clothes. Homily had a similar thought.

"Nothing like a good, strong stream of soapy water running clean through the fabric . . . no rubbing or squeezing; all we've got to do now is lay them out to dry."

They emerged at last, Arrietty running ahead onto a small sandy beach that fanned out sideways and down to the water in front. The mouth of the drain was set well back under the bank of the stream, which overhung it, crowned with rushes and grasses: a sheltered, windless corner on which the sun beat down, rich with the golden promise of an early summer.

"But you can never tell," said Homily gazing around at the weatherworn flotsam and jetsam spewed out by the drain, "not in March . . ."

They had found Pod's bundle just within the mouth of the drain where the hatpin had stuck in the sand. The soapbox lid had fetched up, upside down, against a protruding root, and the egg, Arrietty discovered, had rolled right into the water; it lay in the shallows below a fish-boning of silver ripples and seemed to have flattened out. But when they hooked it onto the dry sand, they saw it was due to refraction of the water: the egg was still its old familiar shape but covered with tiny cracks. Arrietty and Spiller rolled it up the slope to where Pod was unpacking the water-soaked bundles, anxious to see if the mackintosh covering had worked. Triumphantly he laid out the contents one by one on the warm sand. "Dry as a bone . . ." he kept saying.

Homily picked out a change of clothes for each. The jerseys, though clean, were rather worn and stretched: they were the ones she had knitted—so long ago it seemed now—on blunted darning needles when they had lived under the kitchen at Firbank. Arrietty and Homily undressed in the mouth of the drain, but Spiller—although offered a garment of Pod's—would not bother to change. He slid off round the corner of the beach to take a look at his kettle.

When they were dressed and the wet clothes spread out to dry, Homily shelled off the top of the egg. Pod wiped down his precious piece of razor blade, oiled to preserve it against rust, and cut them each a slice. They sat in the sunshine, eating contentedly, watching the ripples of the stream. After a while Spiller joined them. He sat just below them, steaming in the warmth and thoughtfully eating his egg.

"Where is the kettle exactly, Spiller?" asked Arrietty. Spiller jerked his head. "Just round the corner." Pod had packed the Christmas pudding thimble, and they each had a drink of fresh water. Then they packed up the bundles again, and leaving the clothes to dry, they followed Spiller round the bend.

It was a second beach, rather more open, and the kettle lay against the bank at the far end. It lay slightly inclined, as Spiller had found it, wedged in by the twigs and branches washed by the river downstream. It was a corner on which floating things caught up and anchored themselves against a projection of the bank; the river twisted inwards at this point, running quite swiftly just below the kettle where, Arrietty noticed, the water looked suddenly deep.

Beyond the kettle a cluster of brambles growing under the bank hung out over the water—with new leaves growing among the tawny dead ones; some of these older shoots were trailing in the water, and in the tunnel beneath them, Spiller kept his boat.

Arrietty wanted to see the boat first, but Pod was examining the kettle, in the side of which, where it met the base, was a fair-sized circular rust hole.

"That the way in?" asked Pod.

Spiller nodded.

Pod looked up at the top of the kettle. The lid, he noticed, was not quite in, and Spiller had fixed a piece of twine to the knob in the middle of the lid and had slung it over the arched handle above.

"Come inside," he said to Pod. "I'll show you . . ."

They went inside while Arrietty and Homily waited in the sunshine. Spiller appeared again almost immediately at the rust-hole entrance, exclaiming irritably, "Go on, get out. . . ." And, aided by a shove from Spiller's bare foot, a mottled yellow frog leapt through the air and slithered swiftly into the stream. It was followed by two wood lice, which, as they rolled themselves up in balls, Spiller stooped down and picked up from the floor and threw lightly onto the bank above. "Nothing else," he remarked to Homily, grinning, and disappeared again.

Homily was silent a moment and then she whispered to Arrietty, "Don't fancy sleeping in there tonight. . . ."

"We can clean it out," Arrietty whispered back. "Remember the boot," she added.

Homily nodded, rather unhappily. "When do you think he'll get us down to Little Fordham?"

"Soon as he's been upstream to load. He likes the moon full. . . ." Arrietty whispered.

"Why?" whispered Homily.

"He travels mostly at night."

"Oh," said Homily, her expression bewildered and slightly wild.

A metallic sound attracted their attention to the top of the kettle. The lid, they saw, was wobbling on and off, raised and lowered from inside. "According to how you want it . . ." said a voice. "Very ingenious," they heard a second voice reply in curiously hollow tones.

"Doesn't sound like Pod," whispered Homily, looking startled.

"It's because they're in a kettle," explained Arrietty.

"Oh?" said Homily again. "I wish they'd come out."

They came out then, even as she spoke. As Pod stepped down on the flat stone that was used as a doorstep, he looked very pleased. "See that?" he said to Homily.

Homily nodded.

"Ingenious, eh?"

Homily nodded again.

"Now," Pod went on happily, "we're going to take a look at Spiller's boat. What sort of shoes you got on?"

They were old ones Pod had made. "Why?" asked Homily. "Is it muddy?"

"Not that I know of. But if you're going aboard, you don't want to slip. Better go barefoot like Arrietty. . . ."

Chapter Fourteen

Although she seemed nearly aground, a runnel of ice-cold water ran between the boat and the shore; through this they waded, and Spiller, at the prow, helped them to climb aboard. Roomy but clumsy (Arrietty thought as she scrambled in under the legging) but, with her flat bottom, practically impossible to capsize. She was, in fact, as Homily had guessed, a knife box: very long and narrow, with symmetrical compartments for varying sizes of cutlery.

"More what you'd call a barge," remarked Pod, looking about him. A wooden handle rose up inside, to which, he noticed, the legging had been nailed. "Holds her firm," explained Spiller, tapping the roof of the canopy, "say you want to lift up the sides."

The holds were empty at the moment, except for the narrowest. In this Pod saw an amber-colored knitting needle that ran the length of the vessel, a folded square of frayed red blanket, a wafer-thin butter knife of tarnished Georgian silver, and the handle and blade of his old nail scissor.

"So you've still got that?" he said.

"Comes in useful," said Spiller. "Careful," he said as Pod took it up, "I've sharpened it up a bit."

"Wouldn't mind this back," said Pod, a trifle enviously, "say, one day, you got another like it."

"Not so easy to come by," said Spiller, and as though to change the subject, he took up the butter knife. "Found this wedged down a crack in the side . . . does me all right for a paddle."

"Just the thing," said Pod. All the cracks and joins were filled in now, he noticed, as regretfully he put back the nail scissor. "Where did you pick up this knife box in the first place?"

"Lying on the bottom upstream. Full of mud when I spotted her. Bit of a job to salvage. Up by the caravans, that's where she was. Like as not, someone pinched the silver and didn't want the box."

"Like as not," said Pod. "So you sharpened her up?" he went on, staring again at the nail scissor.

"That's right," said Spiller, and stooping swiftly, he snatched up the piece of blanket, "You take this," he said. "Might be chilly in the kettle."

"What about you?" said Pod.

"That's all right," said Spiller. "You take it!"

"Oh," exclaimed Homily, "it's the bit we had in the boot . . ." and then she colored slightly. "I think," she added.

"That's right," said Spiller, "better you take it."

"Well, thanks," said Pod and threw it over his shoulder. He looked around again; the legging, he realized, was both camouflage and shelter. "You done a good job, Spiller. I mean . . . you could live in a boat like this—come wind, say, and wet weather."

"That's right," agreed Spiller, and he began to ease the knitting needle out from under the legging, the knob emerging forward at an angle. "Don't want to hurry you," he said.

Homily seemed taken aback. "You going already?" she faltered.

"Sooner he's gone, sooner he's back," said Pod. "Come on, Homily, all ashore now."

"But how long does he reckon he'll be?"

"What would you put it at, Spiller?" asked Pod. "A couple of days? Three? Four? A week?"

"May be less, may be more," said Spiller. "Depends on the weather. Three nights from now, say, if it's moon-light. . . ."

"But what if we're asleep in the kettle?" said Homily.

"That's all right, Homily; Spiller will *knock*." Pod took her firmly by the elbow. "Come on now, all ashore . . . you too, Arrietty."

As Homily, with Pod's help, was lowered into the water, Arrietty jumped from the side; the wet mud, she noticed, was spangled all over with tiny footprints. They linked arms and stood well back to watch Spiller depart. He unloosed the painter, and paddle in hand, let the boat slide stern foremost from under the brambles. As it glided out into open water, it became unnoticeable suddenly and somehow part of the landscape; it might have been a curl of bark or a piece of floating wood.

It was only when Spiller laid down the paddle and stood up to punt with the knitting needle that he became at all conspicuous. They watched through the brambles as, slowly and painstakingly, leaning at each plunge on his pole, he began to come back upstream. As he came abreast of them, they ran out from the brambles to see better. Shoes in hand, they crossed the beach of the kettle and, to keep up with him, climbed round the bluff at the corner and onto the beach of the drain. There, by a tree root,

which came sharply into deepish water, they waved him a last good-by.

"Wish he hadn't had to go," said Homily, as they made their way back across the sand toward the mouth of the drain.

There lay their clothes, drying in the sun, and as they approached, an iridescent cloud like a flock of birds flew off the top of the egg. "Bluebottles!" cried Homily, running forward; then, relieved, she slackened her steps. They were not bluebottles after all but cleanly burnished river flies, striped gaily with blue and gold. The egg appeared untouched, but Homily blew on it hard and dusted it up with her apron because, she explained, "You never know where they may have put their feet. . . ."

Pod, poking about among the flotsam and jetsam, salvaged the circular cork that Homily had used as a seat. "This'll just about do it . . ." he murmured reflectively.

"Do what?" asked Arrietty idly. A beetle had run out from where the cork had been resting, and stooping, she held it by its shell. She liked beetles: their shiny, clear-cut armor, their mechanical joints and joins. And she liked just a little to tease them: they were so easy to hold by the sharp edge of their wing casings and so anxious to get away.

"One day you'll get bitten . . ." Homily warned her as she folded up the clothes, which still, though dry, smelled faintly and pleasantly of sandalwood, "or stung, or nipped, or whatever they do, and serve you right."

Arrietty let the beetle go. "They don't mind, really," she remarked, watching the horned legs scuttle up the slope and the fine grains of dislodged sand tumbling down behind them.

"And here's a hairpin," exclaimed Pod. It was the one Arrietty had found in the drain, clean-washed now and gleaming. "You know what we should do," he went on, "while we're here, that is?"

"What?" asked Homily.

"Come along here regular like, every morning, and see what the drain's brought down."

"There wouldn't be anything I'd fancy," said Homily, folding the last garment.

"What about a gold ring? Many a gold ring, or so I've heard, gets lost down a drain . . . and you wouldn't say no to a safety pin."

"I'd sooner a safety pin," said Homily, "living as we do now."

They carried the bundles round the bluff onto the beach by the kettle. Homily climbed on the smooth stone that wedged the kettle at an angle and peered in through the rust hole. A cold light shone down from above where the lid was raised by its string: the interior smelled of rust and looked very uninviting.

"What we want now, before sundown," said Pod, "is some good clean dried grass to sleep on. We've got the piece of blanket . . ."

He looked about for some way of climbing the bank. There was a perfect place, as though invented for borrowers, where a cluster of tangled roots hung down from the lip of the cliff that curved deeply in behind them. At some time the stream had risen and washed the roots clean of earth, and they hung in festoons and clusters, elastic but safely anchored. Pod and Arrietty went up, hand over hand; there were handholds and footholds, seats, swings, ladders, ropes. . . . It was a borrowers' gymnasium and almost a disappointment to Arrietty when—so soon—they reached the top.

Here among the jadelike spears of new spring growth were pale clumps of hairlike grasses bleached to the color of tow. . . . Pod reaped these down with his razor blade and Arrietty tied them into sheaves. Homily, below, collected these bundles as they pushed them over the cliff edge and carried them up to the kettle.

When the floor of the kettle was well and truly lined, Pod and Arrietty climbed down. Arrietty peered in through the rust hole: the kettle now smelled of hay. The sun was sinking and the air felt slightly colder. "What we all need now," remarked Homily, "is a good hot drink before bed. . . ." But there was no means of making one, so they got out the egg instead. There was plenty left: they each had a thickish slice, topped up by a leaf of sorrel.

Pod unpacked his length of tarred string, knotted one end securely, and passed the other through the center of the cork. He pulled it tight.

"What's that for?" asked Homily, coming beside him, wiping her hands on her apron (. . . no washing up, thank goodness: she had carried the egg shells down to the water's edge and had thrown them into the stream).

"Can't you guess?" asked Pod. He was trimming the cork now, breathing hard, and beveling the edges.

"To block up the rust hole?"

"That's right," said Pod. "We can pull it tight like some kind of stopper once we're all safely inside. . . ."

Arrietty had climbed up the roots again. They could see her on top of the bank. It was breezier up there and her hair was stirring slightly in the wind. Around her the great grass blades, in gentle motion, crossed and recrossed against the darkening sky.

"She likes it out of doors . . ." said Homily fondly.

"What about you?" asked Pod.

"Well," said Homily after a moment, "I'm not one for insects, Pod, never was. Nor for the simple life—if there is such a thing. But tonight"—she gazed about her at the peaceful scene—"tonight, I feel kind of all right."

"That's the way to talk," said Pod, scraping away with his razor blade.

"Or, it might," said Homily, watching him, "be partly due to that cork."

An owl hooted somewhere in the distance, on a hollow, wobbling note . . . a liquid note, it seemed, falling musically on the dusk. But Homily's eyes widened. "Arrietty—" she called shrilly. "Quickly! Come on down."

They felt snug enough in the kettle—snug and secure, with the cork pulled in and the lid let down. Homily had insisted on the latter precaution. "We won't need to *see*," she explained to Pod and Arrietty, "and we get enough air down the spout."

When they woke in the morning, the sun was up and the kettle felt rather hot. But it was exciting to lift off the lid, hand over hand on the twine, and to see a cloudless sky. Pod kicked out the cork, and they crawled through the rust hole and there again was the beach. . . .

They breakfasted out-of-doors. The egg was wearing down, but there was two-thirds left to go. "And sunshine feeds," said Pod. After breakfast Pod went off with his hatpin to see what had come down the drain; Homily busied herself about the kettle and laid out the blanket to air; Arrietty climbed the roots again to explore the top of the bank. "Keep within earshot," Pod had warned them, "and call out now and again. We don't want accidents at this stage—not before Spiller arrives."

"And we don't want them then," retorted Homily. But she seemed curiously relaxed: there was nothing to do but wait—no housework, no cooking, no borrowing, no planning. "Might as well enjoy ourselves," she reflected and settled herself in the sun on the piece of red blanket. To Pod and Arrietty she seemed to be dozing, but this was not the case at all. Homily was busy daydreaming about a house with front door and windows—a home of their very own. Sometimes it was small and compact, sometimes four stories high. And what about the castle she wondered?

For some reason the thought of the castle reminded her of Lupy. What would they be thinking now—back there in that shuttered house? That we've vanished into thin air—that's what it will seem like to them. Homily imagined Lupy's surprise, the excitement, the conjectures. . . . And, smiling to herself, she half closed her eyes: never would they think of the drain. And never, in their wildest dreams, would they think of Little Fordham. . . .

Two halcyon days went by, but on the third day it rained. Clouds gathered in the morning and by afternoon there was a downpour. At first, Arrietty—avid to stay outdoors—took shelter among the roots under the overhanging bank, but soon the rain drove in on the wind and leaked down from the bank above. The roots became slippery and greasy with mud—so all three of them fled to the drain. "I mean," said Homily as they crouched in the entrance, "at least from here we can see out, which is more than you can say for the kettle."

They moved from the drain, however, when Pod heard a drumming in the distance. "Holmcroft," he exclaimed after listening a moment. "Come on, get moving. . . ." Homily, staring at the gray veil of rain outside, protested that, if they were in for a soaking, they might just as well have it hot as cold.

Chapter Fifteen

It was a good thing they moved, however: the stream had risen almost to the base of the bluff round which they must pass to get to the kettle. Even as it was, they had to wade. The water looked thick and brownish. The delicate ripples had become muscular and fierce, and as they hurried across the second beach, they saw great branches borne on the flood, sinking and rising as the water galloped past.

"Spiller can't travel in this . . ." moaned Homily as they changed their clothes in the kettle. She had to raise her voice against the drumming of the raindrops on the lid. Below them, almost as it might be in their cellar, they heard the thunder of the stream. But the kettle perched on its stone and wedged against the bank felt steady as a citadel. The spout was turned away from the wind and no drop got in through the lid. "Double rim," explained Pod. "Well made, these old fashioned kettles. . . ."

Banking on Spiller's arrival, they had eaten the last of the egg. They felt very hungry and stared with tragic eyes through the rust hole when, just below them, a half loaf went by on the flood.

At last it grew dark and they pulled in the cork and prepared to go to sleep. "Anyway," said Pod, "we're warm and dry. And it's bound to clear up soon. . . ."

But it rained all the next day. And the next. "He'll never come in this," moaned Homily.

"I wouldn't put it past him," said Pod. "That's a good solid craft that knife box, and well covered in. The current flows in close here under those brambles. That's why he chose this corner. You mark my words, Homily, he might fetch up here any moment. Spiller's not one to be frightened by a drop of rain. . . ."

That was the day of the banana. Pod had gone out to reconnoiter, climbing gingerly along the slippery shelf of mud beneath the brambles. The current, twisting in, was pouring steadily through Spiller's boathouse, pulling the trailing brambles in its wake. Caught up in the branches where they touched the water, Pod had found half a packet of sodden cigarettes, a strip of water-logged sacking, and a whole, rather overripe banana.

Homily had screamed when he pushed it in inch by inch through the rust hole. She did not recognize it at first, and later, as she saw what it was, she began to laugh and cry at the same time.

"Steady, Homily," said Pod, after the final push, as he peered in, grave-faced, through the rust hole. "Get a hold on yourself."

Homily did—almost at once. "You should have warned us," she protested, still gasping a little and wiping her eyes on her apron.

"I did call out," said Pod, "but what with the noise of the rain . . ."

They ate their fill of the banana—it was overripe already and would not last for long. Pod sliced it across, skin and all; he thus kept it decently covered. The sound of the rain made talking difficult. "Coming down faster," said Pod. Homily leaned forward, mouthing the words. "Do you think he's met with an accident?"

Pod shook his head. "He'll come when it stops. We got to have patience," he added.

"Have what?" shouted Homily above the downpour.

"Patience," repeated Pod.

"I can't hear you. . . ."

"Patience!" roared Pod.

Rain began to come in down the spout. There was nothing for it but to sacrifice the blanket. Homily stuffed it in as tightly as she could, and the kettle became very airless. "Might go on for a month," she grumbled.

"What?" shouted Pod.

"For a month," repeated Homily.

"What about it?"

"The rain," shouted Homily.

After that they gave up talking: the effort seemed hardly worthwhile. Instead, they lay down in the layers of dried grasses and tried to go to sleep. Full-fed and in that airless warmth, it did not take them long. Arrietty dreamed she was at sea in Spiller's boat: there was a gentle rocking motion, which at first seemed rather pleasant, and then in her dream the boat began to spin. The spinning increased and the boat became a wheel, turning . . . turning. . . . She clung to the spokes, which became like straw and broke away in her grasp. She clung to the rim, which opened outwards and seemed to fling her off, and a voice was calling again and again, "Wake up, Arrietty, wake up. . . ."

Dizzily she opened her eyes, and the kettle seemed full of a whirling half-light. It was morning, she realized, and someone had pulled the blanket from the spout. Close behind her she made out the outline of Pod; he seemed in some strange way to be glued to the side of the kettle. Opposite her she perceived the form of her mother, spread-eagled likewise in the same fixed, curious manner. She herself, half sitting, half lying, felt gripped by some dreamlike force.

"We're afloat," cried Pod, "and spinning." And Arrietty, besides the kettle's spin, was aware of a dipping and swaying. "We've come adrift. We're in the current," he went on, "and going downstream fast. . . ."

"Oh, my . . ." moaned Homily, casting up her eyes. It was the only gesture she could make, stuck as she was like a fly to flypaper. But even as she spoke, the speed slackened and the spinning turns slowed down, and Arrietty watched her mother slide slowly down to a sitting position on the squelching, waterlogged floor. "Oh, my goodness . . ." Homily muttered again.

Her voice, Arrietty noticed, sounded strangely audible: the rain had stopped at last.

"I'm going to get the lid off," said Pod. He, too, as the kettle ceased twisting, had fallen forward to his knees and now rose slowly, steadying himself by a hand on the wall, against the swaying half-turns. "Give me a hand with the twine, Arrietty."

They pulled together. Water had seeped in past the cork in the rust hole and the floor was awash with sodden grass. As they pulled, they slid and slithered, but gradually the lid rose and above them they saw, at last, a circle of bright sky.

"Oh, my goodness," Homily kept saying, and sometimes she changed it to, "Oh, my goodness me. . . ." But she helped them stack up Pod's bundles. "We got to get out on deck like," Pod had insisted. "We don't stand a chance down below."

It was a scramble: they used the twine, they used the hatpin, they used the banana, they used the bundles, and somehow—the kettle listing steeply—they climbed out on the rim to hot sunshine and a cloudless sky. Homily sat crouched, her arms gripped tightly round the stem of the arched handle, her legs dangling below. Arrietty sat beside her holding onto the rim. To lighten the weight, Pod cut the lid free and cast it overboard: they watched it float away.

". . . seems a waste," said Homily.

Chapter Sixteen

The kettle turned slowly as it drifted—more gently now—downstream. The sun stood high in a brilliant sky: it was later than they had thought. The water looked muddy and yellowish after the recent storm, and in some places had overflowed the banks. To the right of them lay open fields and to the left a scrub of stunted willows and taller hazels. Above their heads golden lamb's tails trembled against the sky and armies of rushes marched down into the water.

"Fetch up against the bank any minute now," said Pod hopefully, watching the flow of the stream. "One side or another," he added, "a kettle like this don't drift on forever. . . ."

"I should sincerely hope not," said Homily. She had slightly relaxed her grip on the handle and, interested in spite of herself, was gazing about her.

Once they heard a bicycle bell, and some seconds later a policeman's helmet sailed past just above the level of the bushes. "Oh, my goodness," muttered Homily, "that means a footpath. . . ."

"Don't worry," said Pod. But Arrietty, glancing quickly at her father's face, saw he seemed perturbed.

"He'd only have to glance sideways," Homily pointed out.

"It's all right," said Pod, "he's gone now. And he didn't."

"What about Spiller?" Homily went on.

"What about him?"

"He'll never find us now."

"Why not?" said Pod. "He'll see the kettle's gone. As far as Spiller's concerned, all we've got to do is bide our time, wait quietly—wherever we happen to fetch up."

"Suppose we don't fetch up and go on past Little Fordham?"

"Spiller'll come on past looking for us."

"Suppose we fetch up amongst all those people . . . ?"

"What people?" asked Pod a trifle wearily. "The plaster ones?"

"No, those human beings who swarm about on the paths . . ."

"Now, Homily," said Pod, "no good meeting trouble halfway."

"Trouble?" exclaimed Homily. "What are we in now, I'd like to know?" She glanced down past her knees at the sodden straw below. "And I suppose this kettle'll fill up in no time . . ."

"Not with the cork swollen up like it is," said Pod. "The wetter it gets, the tighter it holds. All you got to do,

Homily, is to sit there and hold on tight; and, say, we come near land, get yourself ready to jump." As he spoke, he was busy making a grappling hook out of his hatpin, twisting and knotting a length of twine about the head of the pin.

Arrietty, meanwhile, lay flat on her stomach gazing into the water below. She was perfectly happy: the cracked enamel was warm from the sun and with one elbow crooked round the base of the handle she felt curiously safe. Once in the turgid water she saw the ghostly outline of a large fish, fanning its shadowy fins and standing backwards against the current. Sometimes there were little forests of water weeds, where blackish minnows flicked and darted. Once a water rat swam swiftly past the kettle, almost under her nose: she called out then excitedly—as though she had seen a whale. Even Homily craned over to watch it pass, admiring the tiny air bubbles that clung like moonstones among the misted fur. They all stood up to watch it climb out on the bank and shake itself hurriedly into a cloud of spray before it scampered away into the grasses. "Well I never," remarked Homily. ". . . natural history," she added reflectively.

Then, raising her eyes, she saw the cow. It stood quite motionless above its own vast shadow, hock deep and silent in the fragrant mud. Homily stared aghast and even Arrietty felt grateful for a smoothly floating kettle and a stretch of water between. Almost impertinently safe

she felt—so near and yet so far—until a sudden eddy in the current swung them in toward the bank.

"It's all right," called Pod as Arrietty started back. "It won't hurt you. . . ."

"Oh, my goodness . . ." exclaimed Homily, making as though to climb down inside the rim. The kettle lurched.

"Steady," cried Pod, alarmed, "keep her trimmed!" And, as the kettle slid swiftly shoreward, he flung his weight sideways, leaning out from the handle. "Stand by . . ." he shouted as with a vicious twist they veered round sharply, gliding against the mud. "Hold fast!" The great cow backed two paces as they careered up under her nose. She lowered her head and swayed slightly as though embarrassed, and then, sniffing the air, she clumsily backed again.

The kettle teetered against the walls and craters of the cow tracks, pressed by the current's flow; a faint vibration of drumming water quivered through the iron. Then Pod, leaning outwards, clinging with one hand to the rim, shoved his hatpin against a stone; the kettle bounced slightly, turning into the current, and, in a series of bumps and quivers, began to turn away.

"Thank goodness for that, Pod . . ." cried Homily, "thank goodness . . . thank goodness . . . oh my, oh my, oh my!" She sat clinging to the base of the handle, white-faced and shaking.

"It would never hurt you," said Pod as they glided out to midstream, "not a cow wouldn't . . ."

"Might tread on us," gasped Homily.

"Not once it's seen you, it wouldn't."

"And it did see us," cried Arrietty gazing backward. "It's looking at us still . . ."

Watching the cow, relaxed and relieved, they were none of them prepared for the bump. Homily, thrown off balance, slid forward with a cry—down through the lid hole onto the straw below. Pod just in time caught hold of the handle rail, and Arrietty caught hold of Pod. Steadying Arrietty, Pod turned his head; the kettle, he saw, had fetched up against an island of sticks and branches, plumb in the middle of the stream. Again the kettle thrummed, banging and trembling against the obstructing sticks; little ripples rose up and broke like waves among and around the weed-strewn, trembling mass.

"Now, we are stuck," remarked Pod, "good and proper."

"Get me up, Pod—do . . ." they heard Homily calling from below.

They got her up and showed her what had happened. Pod, peering down, saw part of a gatepost and coils of rusted wire: on this projection a mass of rubbish was entangled, brought down by the flood, a kind of floating island, knitted up by the current and hopelessly intertwined.

No good shoving with his pin: the current held them head on and, with each successive bump, wedged them more securely.

"It could be worse," remarked Homily surprisingly, when she had got her breath. She took stock of the nest-like structure: some of the sticks, forced above water, had already dried in the sun; the whole contraption, to Homily, looked pleasantly like dry land. "I mean," she went on, "we could walk about on this. I wouldn't say, really, but what I don't prefer it to the kettle . . . better than floating on and on and on, and ending up, as might well be, in the Indian Ocean. Spiller could find us here easy enough . . . plumb in the middle of the view."

"There's something in that," agreed Pod. He glanced up at the banks: the stream here was wider, he noticed. On the left bank, among the stunted willows that shrouded the towpath, a tall hazel leaned over the water; on the right bank, the meadows came sloping down to the stream and, beside the muddy cow tracks, stood a sturdy clump of ash. The tall boles, ash and hazel, stood like sentinels, one each side of the river. Yes, it was the kind of spot Spiller would know well; the kind of place, Pod thought to himself, to which humans might give a name. The water on either side of the midstream obstruction flowed dark and deep, scooped out by the current into pools. Yes, it was the kind of place he decided—with a slight inward tremor of his "feeling"—where in the summer human beings might come to bathe. Then, glancing downstream, he saw the bridge.

Chapter Seventeen

It was not much of a bridge—wooden, moss-grown, with a single handrail—but, in their predicament, even a modest bridge was still a bridge too many: bridges are highways, built for humans, and command long views of the river . . .

Homily, when he pointed it out, seemed strangely unperturbed: shading her eyes against the sunlight, she gazed intently down river. "No human being that distance away," she decided at last, "could make out what's on these sticks. . . ."

"You'd be surprised," said Pod. "They spot the movement like . . ."

"Not before we've spotted them. Come on, Pod; let's unload the kettle and get some stuff dried out."

They went below, and by shifting the ballast, they got the kettle well heeled over. When they had achieved sufficient list, Pod took his twine and made the handle fast to the sunken wire netting. In this way, with the kettle held firm, they could crawl in and out through the lid hole.

Soon all the gear was spread out in the warmth, and sitting in a row on a baked branch of alder, they each fell to on a slice of banana.

"This could be a lot worse," said Homily, munching and looking about her. She was thankful for the silence and the sudden lack of motion. Down between the tangled sticks were well-like glintings of dark water, but it was quiet water and, from her high perch, far enough away to be ignored.

Arrietty, on the contrary, had taken off her shoes and stockings and was trailing her feet in the delicate ripples that played about the outer edges.

The river seemed full of voices, endless, mysterious murmurs like half-heard conversations. But conversations without pauses—breathless, steady recountings. . . . "She said to me, I said to her. And then . . . and then . . . and then. . . ." After a while Arrietty ceased to listen as, so often, she ceased to listen to her mother when Homily, in the vein, went on and on and on. But she was aware of the sound and the deadening effect it would have on sounds made farther afield. Against this noise, she thought, something could creep up on you and, without hint or warning, suddenly be there. And then she realized that nothing could creep up on an island unless it were afloat or could swim. But, even as she thought this thought, a blue tit flew down from above and perched beside her on a twig. It cocked its head sideways at the pale ring of banana skin that had enclosed her luncheon slice.

She picked it up and threw it sideways toward him—like a quoit—and the blue tit flew away.

Then she crept back into the nest of flotsam. Sometimes she climbed under the dry twigs onto the wet ones below. In these curious hollows, cut with sunlight and shadow,

there was a vast choice of handholds and notches on which to tread. Above her a network of branches crisscrossed against the sun. Once she went right down to the shadowed water and, hanging perilously above it, saw in its blackness her pale reflected face. She found a water snail

clinging to the underside of a leaf, and once, with a foot, she touched some frogs' spawn, disturbing a nest of tadpoles. She tried to pull up a water weed by the roots but, slimily, it resisted her efforts—stretching part way like a piece of elasticized rubber, then suddenly springing free.

"Where are you, Arrietty?" Homily called from above. "Come up here where it's dry. . . ."

But Arrietty seemed not to hear: she had found a hen's feather, a tuft of sheep's wool, and half a ping-pong ball, which still smelled strongly of celluloid. Pleased with these borrowings, she finally emerged. Her parents were suitably impressed, and Homily made a cushion of the sheep's wool, wedged it neatly in the half-ball, and used it as a seat. "And very comfortable too," she assured them warmly, wobbling slightly on the curved base.

Once two small humans crossed the bridge, country boys of nine or ten. They dawdled and laughed and climbed about and threw sticks into the water. The borrowers froze, staring intently as, with backs turned, the two boys hung on the railings, watching their sticks drift downstream.

"Good thing we're upstream," murmured Pod from between still lips.

The sun was sinking and the river had turned to molten gold. Arrietty screwed up her eyelids against the glitter. "Even if they saw us," she whispered, her eyes on the bridge, "they couldn't get at us—out here in deep water."

"Maybe not," said Pod, "but the word would get around. . . ."

The boys at length disappeared. But the borrowers remained still, staring at the bushes and trying to hear above the bubble of the river any sound of human beings passing along the footpath.

"I think they must have gone across the fields," said Pod at last. "Come on, Arrietty, give me a hand with this waterproof. . . ."

Pod had been preparing a hammock bed for the night where four stout sticks lay lengthwise in a hollow: a mackintosh ground sheet, their dry clothes laid out on top, the piece of lamb's wool for a pillow and, to cover them, another ground sheet above the piece of red blanket. Snug, they would be, in a deep cocoon—protected from rain and dew and invisible from the bank.

As the flood water began to subside, their island seemed to rise higher; slimy depths were revealed among the structure, and gazing down between the sticks at the rusted wire, they discovered a waterlogged shoe.

"Nothing to salvage there," remarked Pod after a moment's thoughtful silence, "except maybe the laces. . . ."

Homily, who had followed them downwards, gazed wonderingly about her. It had taken courage to climb down into the depths. She had tested every foothold: some of the branches were rotten and broke away at a touch; others less securely wedged were apt to become detached, and quivers and slidings took place elsewhere—like a distant disturbance in a vast erection of spilikins. Their curious island was only held together, she realized, by the interrelation of every leaf, stick, and floating strand of weed. All the same, on the way up, she snapped off a living twig of hawthorn for the sake of the green leaf buds. "A bit of salad like, to eat with our supper," she explained to Arrietty. "You can't go on forever just on egg and banana. . . ."

Chapter Eighteen

They ate their supper on the upstream side of the island, where the ripples broke at their feet and where the kettle, tied on its side, had risen clear of the water. The level of the stream was sinking fast and the water seemed far less muddy.

It was not much of a supper—the tail end of the banana that had become rather sticky. They still felt hungry, even after they had finished off the hawthorn shoots, washing them down with draughts of cold water. They spoke wistfully of Spiller and a boat chock-full of borrowings.

"Suppose we miss him?" said Homily. "Suppose he comes in the night?"

"I'll keep watch for Spiller," said Pod.

"Oh, Pod," exclaimed Homily, "you've got to have your eight hours!"

"Not tonight," said Pod, "nor tomorrow night. Nor any night while there's a full moon."

"We could take it in turns," suggested Homily.

"I'll watch tonight," said Pod, "and we'll see how we go."

Homily was silent, staring down at the water. It was a dreamlike evening: as the moon rose, the warmth of the day still lingered on the landscape in a glow of tranquil light. Colors seemed enriched from within, vivid but softly muted.

"What's that?" said Homily suddenly, gazing down at the ripples. "Something pink . . ."

They followed the direction of her eyes. Just below the surface something wriggled, held up against the current.

"It's a worm," said Arrietty after a moment.

Homily stared at it thoughtfully. "You said right, Pod," she admitted after a moment. "I have changed. . . ."

"In what way?" asked Pod.

"Looking at that worm," said Homily, "all scoured and scrubbed like—clean as a whistle—I was thinking"—she hesitated—"well, I was thinking . . . I could eat a worm like that. . . ."

"What, raw?" exclaimed Pod, amazed.

"No, stewed of course," retorted Homily crossly, "with a bit of wild garlic." She stared again at the water. "What's it caught up on?"

Pod craned forward. "I can't quite see . . ." Suddenly his face became startled and his gaze, sharply intent, slid away on a rising curve toward the bushes.

"What's the matter, Pod?" asked Homily.

He looked at her aghast—a slow stare. "Someone's fishing," he breathed, scarcely above his breath.

"Where?" whispered Homily.

Pod jerked his head toward the stunted willows. "There —behind those bushes . . ."

Then Homily, raising her eyes at last, made out the fishing line. Arrietty saw it too. Only in glimpses was it visible: not at all under water but against the surface here and there they perceived the hair-thin shadow. As it rose, it became invisible again, lost against the dimness of the willows, but they could follow its direction.

"Can't see nobody," whispered Homily.

"Course you can't," snapped Pod. "A trout's got eyes, remember, just like you and me. . . ."

"Not *just* like—" protested Homily.

"You don't want to show yourself," Pod went on, "not when you're fishing."

"Especially if you're poaching," put in Arrietty. Why are we whispering, she wondered—our voices can't be heard above the voices of the river?

"That's right, lass," said Pod, "especially if you're poaching. And that's just what he is, I shouldn't wonder —a poacher."

"What's a poacher?" whispered Homily.

Pod hushed her, raising his hand. "Quiet, Homily." And then he added aside, "a kind of human borrower."

"A human borrower . . ." repeated Homily in a bewildered whisper: it seemed a contradiction in terms.

"Quiet, Homily," pleaded Pod.

"He can't hear us," said Arrietty, "not from the bank. Look—" she exclaimed. "The worm's gone."

So it had, and the line had gone too.

"Wait a minute," said Pod. "You'll see—he sends **it** down on the current."

Straining their eyes, they made out the curves of floating line and, just below the surface, the pinkness of the worm sailing before them. The worm fetched up in the same spot, just below their feet, where again it was held against the current.

Something flicked out from under the sticks below them; there was a flurry of shadow, a swift half-turn, and most of the worm had gone.

"A fish?" whispered Arrietty.

Pod nodded.

Homily craned forward: she was becoming quite excited. "Look, Arrietty—now you can see the hook!"

Arrietty caught just a glimpse of it and then the hook was gone.

"He felt that," said Pod, referring to the fisherman. "Thinks he got a bite."

"But he did get a bite," said Arrietty.

"He got a bite but he didn't get a fish. Here it comes again. . . ."

It was a new worm this time, darker in color.

Homily shuddered. "I wouldn't fancy that one, whichever way you cooked it."

"Quiet, Homily," said Pod as the worm whisked away.

"You know," exclaimed Homily excitedly, "what **we** could do—say we had some kind of fire. We could take the fish off the hook and cook and eat it ourselves. . . ."

"Say there was a fish *on* the hook—" remarked Pod, gazing soberly toward the bushes. Suddenly he gave a cry and ducked sideways, his hands across his face. "Look out!" he yelled in a frantic voice.

It was too late: there was the hook in Homily's skirt, worm and all. They ran to her, holding her against the pull of the line while her wild shrieks echoed down the river.

"Unbutton it, Homily! Take the skirt off! Quick . . ."

But Homily couldn't or wouldn't. It might have had something to do with the fact that underneath she was wearing a very short red flannel petticoat that once had belonged to Arrietty and did not think it would look seemly, or she might quite simply just have lost her head. She clung to Pod, and dragged out of his grasp, she clung to Arrietty. Then she clung to the twigs and sticks as she was dragged past them toward the ripples.

They got her out of the water as the line for a moment went slack, and Arrietty fumbled with the small jet bead that served Homily's skirt as a button. Then the line went taut again. As Pod grabbed hold of Homily, he saw out of the corner of his eye that the fisherman was standing up.

From this position, on the very edge of the bank, he could play his rod more freely. A sudden upward jerk, and Homily, caught by her skirt and shrieking loudly, flew upside down into the air with Pod and Arrietty

fiercely clinging each to an arm. Then the jet button
burst off, the skirt sailed away with the worm, and the
borrowers, in a huddle, fell back on the sticks. The sticks

sank slightly beneath the impact and rose again as gently,
breaking the force of their fall.

"That was a near one," gasped Pod, pulling his leg out
of a cleft between the branches. Arrietty, who had come
down on her seat, remained sitting: she seemed shaken but
unhurt. Homily, crossing her arms, tenderly massaged

her shoulders: she had a long graze on one cheek and a jagged tear in the red flannel petticoat. "You all right, Homily?"

Homily nodded, and her bun unrolled slowly. White-faced and shaking, she felt mechanically for hairpins: she was staring fixedly at the bank.

"And the sticks held," said Pod, examining his grazed shin: he swung the leg slightly. "Nothing broken," he said. Homily took no notice: she sat, as though mesmerized, staring at the fisherman.

"It's Mild Eye," she announced grimly after a moment.

Pod swung round, narrowing his eyes. Arrietty stood up to see better: Mild Eye, the gypsy . . . there was no mistaking the apelike build, the heavy eyebrows, the thatch of graying hair.

"Now we'll be for it," said Homily.

Pod was silent a moment. "He can't get at us here," he decided at last, "right out in midstream; the water's goo and deep out here, on both sides of us like."

"He could stand in the shallows and reach," said Homily.

"Doubt if he'd make it," said Pod.

"He knows us and he's seen us," said Homily in the same expressionless voice. She drew a long, quivering breath. "And, you mark my words, he's not going to miss again!"

There was silence except for the voices of the river. The babbling murmur, unperturbed and even, seemed suddenly alien and heartless.

"Why doesn't he move?" asked Arrietty.

"He's thinking," said Homily.

After a moment Arrietty ventured timidly, "Of what he's going to charge for us, and that, when he's got us in a cage?"

"Of what he's going to do next," said Homily.

They were silent a moment, watching Mild Eye.

"Look," said Arrietty.

"What's he up to now?" asked Pod.

"He's taking the skirt off the hook!"

"And the worm too," said Pod. "Look out!" he cried as the fisherman's arm flew up. There was a sudden jerk among the sticks, a shuddering series of elastic quivers. "He's casting for us," shouted Pod. "Better we get under cover."

"No," said Homily, as their island became still again; she watched the caught branch, hooked loose, bobbing away down river. "Say he drags this obstruction to bits, we're safer on top than below. Better we take to the kettle—"

But even as she spoke, the next throw caught the cork in the rust hole. The kettle, hooked by its stopper and tied to the sticks, resisted the drag of the rod: they clung together in silent panic as just below them branches began to slide. Then the cork bounced free and leapt away, dancing on the end of the line. Their island subsided again, and unclasping each other, they moved apart listening wide-eyed to the rhythmic gurgle of water filling the kettle.

The next throw caught a key branch, one on which they stood. They could see the hook well and truly in, and the trembling strain on the twine. Pod clambered alongside and, leaning back, tugged downwards against the pull. But strain as he might, the line stayed taut and the hook as deeply embedded.

"Cut it," cried someone above the creaking and groaning. "Cut it . . ." the voice cried again, tremulously faint, like the rippling voice of the river.

"Then give me the razor blade," gasped Pod. Arrietty brought it in a breathless scramble. There was a gentle twang, and they all ducked down as the severed line flew free. "Now why," exclaimed Pod, "didn't I think of that in the first place?"

He glanced toward the shore. Mild Eye was reeling in; the line, too light now, trailed softly on the breeze.

"He's not very pleased," said Homily.

"No," agreed Pod, sitting down beside her, "he wouldn't be."

"Don't think he's got another hook," said Homily.

They watched Mild Eye examine the end of his line, and they met his baleful gaze as, throwing the rod aside, he angrily stared across at them.

"Round one to us," said Pod.

Chapter Nineteen

They settled themselves more comfortably, preparing for a vigil. Homily reached behind her into the bedding and pulled out the piece of red blanket. "Look, Pod," she said in an interested voice as she tucked it around her knees, "what's he up to now?" They watched intently as Mild Eye, taking up his rod again, turned toward the bushes. "You don't think he's given it up?" she added as Mild Eye, making for the towpath, disappeared from view.

"Not a hope," said Pod, "not Mild Eye. Not once he's seen us and knows we're here for the taking."

"He can't get at us here," said Homily again, "and it'll be dark soon." She seemed strangely calm.

"Maybe," said Pod, "but look at that moon rising. And we'll still be here in the morning." He took up his razor blade. "Might as well free that kettle: it's only a weight on the sticks. . . ."

Homily watched him slice through the twine, and, a little sadly, they watched the kettle sink.

"Poor Spiller," said Arrietty, "he was kind of fond of that kettle. . . ."

"Well, it served its purpose," said Pod.

"What if we made a raft?" suggested Homily suddenly. Pod looked about at the sticks and down at the twine in his hand. "We could do," he said, "but it would take a bit of time. And with him about"—he jerked his head toward the bushes—"I reckon we're as safe here as anywhere."

"And it's better here," said Arrietty, "for being seen."

Homily, startled, turned and looked at her. "Whatever do you want to be seen for?"

"I was thinking of Spiller," said Arrietty. "With this kind of moon and this sort of weather, he'll come tonight most likely."

"Pretty well bound to," agreed Pod.

"Oh dear," said Homily, pulling the blanket around her, "whatever will he think? I mean, finding me like this —in Arrietty's petticoat?"

"Nice and bright," said Pod, "catch his eye nicely, that petticoat would."

"Not short and shrunk up like it is," complained Homily unhappily, "and a great tear in the side like."

"It's still bright," said Pod, "a kind of landmark. And I'm sorry now we sunk the kettle. He'd have seen that too. Well, can't be helped. . . ."

"Look—" whispered Arrietty, gazing at the bank.

There stood Mild Eye. Just beside them he seemed now:

he had walked down the towpath behind the bushes and had emerged on the bank beside the leaning hazel. In the clear shadowless light he seemed extraordinarily close: they could even see the pallor of his one blue eye in contrast to the fiercely shadowed black one; they could see the joints in his fishing rod and the clothes pegs and coils of clothesline in his basket, which he carried half slung on his forearm and tilted toward them. Had it been dry land between them, four good strides would have brought him across.

"Oh dear," muttered Homily, "now what?"

Mild Eye, leaning his rod against the hazel, set down the basket from which he took two fair-sized fish strung together by the gills. These he wrapped carefully in several layers of dock leaves.

"Rainbow trout," said Arrietty.

"How do you know?" asked Homily.

Arrietty blinked her eyelids. "I just know," she said.

"Young Tom," said Pod, "that's how she knows, I reckon—seeing his granddad's the gamekeeper. And that's how she knew about poachers, eh, Arrietty?"

Arrietty did not reply: she was watching Mild Eye as he returned the fish to the basket. Very carefully he seemed to be placing them, deep among the clothes pegs. He then took up two coils of clothesline and laid these carelessly on top.

Arrietty laughed. "As if," she whispered scornfully, "they wouldn't search his basket!"

"Quiet, Arrietty," said Homily, watching intently as Mild Eye, staring across at them, advanced to the edge of the bank. "It's early yet to laugh. . . ."

On the edge of the bank Mild Eye sat down and, his eyes still fixed on the borrowers, began to unlace his boots.

"Oh, Pod," moaned Homily suddenly, "you see those boots? They are the same, aren't they? I mean—to think we lived in one of them! Which was it, Pod, left or right?"

"The one with the patch," said Pod, alert and watching. "He won't make it," he added throughtfully, "not by paddling."

"Think of him wearing a boot patched up by you, Pod."

"Quiet, Homily—" pleaded Pod as Mild Eye, barefoot by now, began to roll up his trousers. "Get ready to move back."

"And me getting *fond* of that boot!" exclaimed Homily just above her breath. She seemed fascinated by the pair of them, set neatly together now, on the grassy verge of the stream.

They watched as Mild Eye, a hand on the leaning hazel, lowered himself into the water. It came to just above his ankles. "Oh, my," muttered Homily, "it's shallow. Better we move back. . . ."

"Wait a minute," said Pod. "You watch!"

The next step took Mild Eye in to well above the knee,

wetting the turnup of his trousers. He stood, a little non-plussed, holding tight to the leaning branch of the hazel.

"Bet it's cold," whispered Arrietty.

Mild Eye stared as though measuring the distance between them, and then he glanced back at the bank. Sliding his hand farther out along the branch, he took a second step. This brought him in almost to the thigh. They saw him start as the coldness of the water seeped through his trousers to his skin. He glanced at the branch above. It was already bending; he could not with safety move farther. Then, his free arm outstretched toward them, he began to lean. . . .

"Oh, my—" moaned Homily, as the swarthy face came nearer. The outstretched fingers had a greedy steadiness about them. Reaching, reaching . . .

"It's quite all right," said Pod.

It was as though Mild Eye heard him. The black eye widened slightly while the blue one smoothly stared. The stream moved gently past the soaking corduroys. They could hear the gypsy's breathing.

Pod cleared his throat. "You can't do it," he said. Again the black eye widened and Mild Eye opened his mouth. He did not speak, but his breathing became even deeper and he glanced again at the shore. Then clumsily he began to retreat, clinging to his branch, and feeling backwards with his feet for rising ground on the slimy bottom. The branch creaked ominously under his weight and, once in

shallower water, he quickly let it go and splashed back unaided to the bank. He stood there dripping and gasping and staring at them heavily. There was still no expression on his face. After a while he sat down; and rather unsteadily, still staring, he rolled himself a cigarette.

Chapter Twenty

"I told you he couldn't make it," said Pod. "Needed a good half yard or another couple of feet. . . ." He patted Homily on the arm. "All we've got to do now is to hold out till dark, and Spiller will come for sure."

They sat in a row on the same stick, facing upstream. To watch Mild Eye, they had to turn slightly sideways to the left.

"Look at him now," whispered Homily. "He's still thinking."

"Let him think," said Pod.

"Supposing Spiller came now?" suggested Arrietty, gazing hopefully along the water.

"He couldn't do anything," said Pod, "not under Mild Eye's nose. Say he did come now, he'd see we were all right like and he'd take cover near until dark. Then he'd bring his boat alongside on the far side of the island and take us all aboard. That's what I reckon he'd do."

"But it won't ever get dark," Arrietty protested, "not with a full moon."

"Moon or no moon," said Pod, "Mild Eye won't sit there all night. He'll be getting peckish soon. And as far as he calculates, he's got us all tied up like and safe to leave for morning. He'll come along then, soon as it's light, with all the proper tackle."

"What is the proper tackle?" asked Homily uneasily.

"I hope," said Pod, "that not being here, we won't never need to know."

"How does he know we can't swim?" asked Arrietty.

"For the same reason as we know he can't: if he could've swum, he'd have swum. And the same applies to us."

"Look," said Arrietty, "he's standing up again . . . he's getting something out of the basket!"

They watched intently as Mild Eye, cigarette dangling out of the corner of his mouth, fumbled among the clothes pegs.

"Oh my," said Homily, "see what's he doing? He's got a coil of clothesline. Oh, I don't like this, Pod. This looks to me"—she caught her breath—"a bit like the proper tackle."

"Stay quiet and watch," said Pod.

Mild Eye, cigarette in mouth, was deliberately unfolding several lengths of line, which, new and stiff, hung in curious angles. Then, an end of rope in his hand, he stared at the trunk of the hazel. "I see what he's going to do," breathed Homily.

"Quiet, Homily—we all see. But"—Pod narrowed his

eyes, watching intently as Mild Eye attached the length of rope above a branch high on the trunk of the hazel—"I can't quite figure where it gets him. . . ."

Climbing down off a curve of root, Mild Eye pulled on the rope, testing the strength of the knot. Then, turning toward them, he gazed across the river. They all turned round, following the direction of his eyes. Homily gasped. "He's going to tie the other end to that ash tree. . . ." Instinctively she ducked as the coil of rope came sailing above their heads and landed on the opposite bank. The slack of rope, missing their island by inches, trailed on the surface of the water. "Wish we could get at it," muttered Homily, but, even as she spoke, the current widened the loop and carried it farther away. The main coil seemed caught in the brambles below the alder. Mild Eye had disappeared again. He emerged, at last, a long way farther down the towpath almost beside the bridge.

"Can't make out what he's up to," said Homily, as Mild Eye, barefoot still, hurried across the bridge, "throwing that rope across. What's he going to do—walk the tightrope or something?"

"Not exactly," said Pod. "The other way round like: it's a kind of overhead bridge as you might say, and you get across by handholds. Done it myself once, from a chair back to lamp table."

"Well, you need both hands for that," exclaimed Homily. "I mean, he couldn't pick us up on the way. Unless he does it with his feet . . ."

"He doesn't need to get right across," explained Pod. He sounded rather worried. "He just needs something to hang onto that's a bit longer than that hazel branch, something he knows won't give way. He just wants a bit more reach, a bit more safe lean-over. . . . He was pretty close to us that time he waded, remember?"

"Yes . . ." said Homily uneasily, watching as Mild Eye picked his way rather painfully along the left bank and made toward the ash tree. "That field's full of stubble," she remarked after a moment.

The rope flew up, scattering them with drops, as Mild Eye pulled it level and made it fast. It quivered above them, still dripping slightly—taut, straight, and very strong-looking. "Bear a couple of men his weight," said Pod.

"Oh, my goodness . . ." whispered Homily.

They stared at the ash tree: a cut end of clothesline hung the length of the bole, still swinging slightly from Mild Eye's efforts. "Knows how to tie a knot . . ." remarked Homily.

"Yes," agreed Pod, looking even more glum. "You wouldn't undo that in a hurry."

Mild Eye took his time walking back. He paused on the bridge and stared awhile up the river as though to admire his handiwork; confident, he seemed suddenly, and in no particular hurry.

"Can he see us from there?" asked Homily, narrowing her eyes.

"I doubt it," said Pod, "not if we're still. Might get a glimpse of the petticoat . . ."

"Not that it matters either way," said Homily.

"No, it don't matter now," said Pod. "Come on now," he added as Mild Eye left the bridge and behind the bushes was starting along the towpath. "What we better do, I reckon, is get over to the far side of the island and each of us straddle a good thick twig: something to hold onto. He may make it and he may not, but we got to keep steady now, all three of us, and take our chance. There ain't nothing else we can do."

They each chose a thickish twig, picking the ones that seemed light enough to float and sufficiently furnished with handholds. Pod helped Homily, who was trembling so violently that she could hardly keep her balance. "Oh, Pod," she moaned, "I don't know what I feel like— perched up here on my own. Wish we could all be together."

"We'll be close enough," said Pod. "And maybe he won't even get within touching distance. Now you hold tight and, no matter what happens, don't you let go. Not even if you end up in the water."

Arrietty sat on her twig as though it were a bicycle: there were two footholds and places for both hands. She felt curiously confident: if the twig broke loose, she felt, she could hold on with her hands and use her feet as paddles. "You know," she explained to her mother, "like a water beetle. . . ." But Homily who, in shape, was more like a water beetle than any of them, did not seem comforted.

Pod took his seat on a knobbly branch of elder. "And make for this far bank," he said, jerking his head toward the ash tree, "if you find you can make for anywhere. See that piece of rope he's left dangling? Well, we might make a grab at that. Or some of those brambles where they trail down into the water . . . get a hold on one of them. Depends where you fetch up . . ."

They were high enough to see across the sticks of their island, and Homily, from her perch, had been watching Mild Eye. "He's coming now," she said grimly. In her dead, expressionless voice there was a dreadful kind of calm.

They saw that this time he laid both hands on the rope and lowered himself more easily into the water. Two careful steps brought him thigh-deep on his foremost leg; here he seemed to hesitate. "Only wants that other couple of feet," said Pod.

Mild Eye moved his foremost hand from the rope and, leaning carefully, stretched out his arm toward them. He waggled his fingers slightly, calculating distance. The rope, which had been so taut, sagged a little under his weight and the leaves of the hazel rustled. He glanced behind him, as he had done before, and seemed reassured by the lissome strength of the tree; but the light was fading, and from across where they waited, they could not see his expression. Somewhere in the dusk a cow lowed sadly and they heard a bicycle bell. If only Spiller would come . . .

Mild Eye, sliding his grasp forward, steadied himself a moment and took another step. He seemed to go in deep, but he was so close now that the height of their floating island hid him from the waistline down. They could no longer see the stretching fingers, but they heard the sticks creak and felt the movement: he was drawing their island toward him.

"Oh, Pod," cried Homily, as she felt the merciless pull of that unseen hand and the squeakings and scrapings below her, "you've been so good to me. All your life you've been so good. I never thought to tell you, Pod—never once—how good you've always been . . ."

She broke off sharply as the island lurched, caught on the barbed-wire obstruction, and, terror-stricken, clutched at her twig. There was a dull crack and two outside branches dislodged themselves slowly and bobbed away downstream.

"You all right, Homily?" called Pod.

"So far," she gasped.

Then everything seemed to happen at once. She saw Mild Eye's expression turn to utter surprise as, lurching forward to grab their island, he pitched face downwards into the water. They went down with him in one resounding splash—or rather, as it seemed to Homily, the water rushed up to them. She had opened her mouth to scream but closed it just in time. Bubbles streamed past her face and tendrils of clinging weed. The water was icily cold but alive with noise and movement. No sooner had she let go her twig, which seemed to be dragging her down, than the hold on the sticks was released and the island rushed up again. Gasping and coughing, Homily broke surface; she saw the trees again, the rising moon, and the dim, rich evening sky. Loudly she called out for Pod.

"I'm here," cried a choked voice from somewhere behind her. There was a sound of coughing. "And Arrietty too. Hold tight, like I said! The island's moving . . ."

The island swung, as though on a pivot, caught by one end on the wire. They were circling round in a graceful curve toward the bank of the ash tree. Homily realized, as she grabbed for a handhold, that Mild Eye in falling had pushed on their floating sticks.

They stopped a little short of the bank, and Homily could see the trailing brambles and the trunk of the ash tree with its piece of hanging cord. She saw Pod and Arrietty had clambered down to the sticks that were nearest the shore, at which, with their backs to Homily, they seemed to be staring intently. As she made her way toward them, slipping and sliding on the wet branches, she heard Arrietty talking excitedly, clutching her father by the arm. "It is . . ." she kept saying, "it is . . ."

Pod turned as Homily approached to help her across the sticks. He seemed preoccupied and rather dazed. A long piece of weed hung down his back in a slimy kind of pigtail. "What's the matter, Pod? You all right?"

Behind them they heard bellows of fright as Mild Eye, emerging from the depths, struggled to find a foothold. Homily, alarmed, gripped Pod by the arm. "It's all right," he told her. "He won't bother with us. Not again tonight at any rate . . ."

"What happened, Pod? The rope broke—or what? Or was it the tree?"

"Seemingly," said Pod, "it were the rope. But I can't see how. Hark at Arrietty." He nodded toward the bank. "She says it's Spiller's boat . . ."

"Where?"

"There under the brambles."

Homily, steadying herself by clinging to Pod, peered forward. The bank was very close now—barely a foot away.

"It is, I know it is," cried Arrietty again, "that thing under there like a log."

"It's like a log," said Pod, "because it is a log."

"Spiller!" called Homily on a gentle rising note, peering into the brambles.

"No good," said Pod, "we've been calling. And, say it was his boat, he'd answer. Spiller—" he called again in a vehement whisper. "You there?"

There was no reply.

"What's that?" cried Pod, turning. A light had flashed on the opposite bank somewhere near the towpath. "Someone's coming," he whispered. Homily heard the sudden jangle of a bicycle and the squeak of brakes as it skidded to a stop. Mild Eye had ceased his swearing and his spitting and, though still in the water, it seemed he had ceased to move. The silence was absolute, except for the running of the river. Homily, about to speak, felt a warning grip on her arm. "Quiet," whispered Pod. A human being on the opposite bank was crashing through the bushes. The light flashed on again and circled about: this time it seemed more blinding, turning the dusk into darkness.

"Hallo . . . hallo . . . hallo . . . 'allo . . ." said a voice. It was a young voice, both stern and gay. It was a voice that seemed familiar to Homily, though, for the moment, she could not put a name to it. Then she remembered that last day at Firbank, under the kitchen floor: the goings on above and the ordeal down below. It was the voice, she realized, of Mrs. Driver's old enemy— Ernie Runacre, the policeman.

She turned to Pod. "Quiet!" he warned her again as the circle of light trembled across the water. On the sticks— if none of them moved—he knew they would not be seen. Homily, in spite of this, gave a sudden loud gasp. "Oh, Pod—" she exclaimed.

"Hush," urged Pod, tightening his grip on her arm.

"It's our nail scissor," persisted Homily, dropping her voice to a breathy kind of whisper. "You must look, Pod. Halfway down the ash tree . . ."

Pod swiveled his eyes round: there it hung, glittering against the bark. It seemed attached in some way to the spare end of rope that Mild Eye had left dangling.

"Then it was Spiller's boat," Arrietty whispered excitedly.

"Keep quiet, can't you—" begged Pod through barely opened lips, "till he shifts the beam of the light!"

But Ernie Runacre, on the opposite bank, seemed taken up with Mild Eye. "Now then," they heard him say in the same brisk policeman's voice, "what's going on here?" And the light beam flicked away to concentrate on the gypsy.

Pod drew a sigh of relief. "That's better," he said, relaxing slightly and using his normal voice.

"But where is Spiller?" fussed Homily, her teeth chattering with cold. "Maybe he's met with an accident."

"But that was Spiller," put in Arrietty eagerly, "coming down the tree with the nail scissor. He'd have it slung by the handle on his shoulder."

"You mean you saw him?"

"No, you don't see Spiller. Not when he doesn't want you to."

"He'd kind of match up with the bark," explained Pod.

"Then if you didn't see him," said Homily after a moment, "how can you be certain?"

"Well, you can't be certain," agreed Pod.

Homily seemed perturbed. "You think it was Spiller cut the rope?"

"Seemingly," said Pod. "Shinned up the tree by that loose bit of leftover. Like I used to with my name tape, remember?"

Homily peered at the brambles. "Say that is his boat under there, which I doubt—why didn't he just come and fetch us?"

"Like I told you," said Pod wearily, "he was laying up till dark. Use your head, Homily. Spiller needs this river— it's his livelihood, like. True, he might have got us off. But—say he was spotted by Mild Eye: he'd be marked down by the gypsies from then on—boat and all. See what I mean? They'd be on the watch for him. Sometimes," Pod went on, "you don't talk like a borrower. You and Arrietty both—you go on at times as though you never heard about cover and such-like, let alone about being seen. You go on, the both of you, like a couple of human beings. . . ."

"Now, Pod," protested Homily, "no need to get insulting."

"But I mean it," said Pod. "And as far as Spiller knew, we was all right here till dark. Once the hook had gone."

They were quiet a moment, listening to the splashes across the water. Homily, caught by the sound of that brisk, familiar voice, moved away from Pod in order to hear what was happening. "Come on, now," Ernie Runacre was saying, "get your foot on that root. That's right. Give us your hand. . . . Bit early, I'd say, for a dip. Wouldn't choose it myself. Sooner try me hand at a bit of fishing . . . providing, of course, I weren't too particular about the bylaws. Come on now"—he caught his breath as though to heave—"one, two, three—hup! Well, there you are! Now, let's take a look at this basket. . . ."

Homily, to get a glimpse of them, had hauled herself up on a twig when she felt Pod's hand on her arm. "Watch," she exclaimed excitedly, gripping his fingers with hers, "he'll find that borrowed fish! That rainbow trout or whatever it's called. . . ."

"Come on, now," whispered Pod.

"Just a minute, Pod—"

"But he's waiting," insisted Pod. "Better we go now, he says, while they're taken up with that basket. . . . And that light on the bank, he says, will make the river seem darker."

Homily turned slowly: there was Spiller's boat, bobbing alongside, with Spiller and Arrietty in the stern. She saw their faces, pale against the shadows, lit by the rising moon. All was quiet, except for the running of the ripples.

Dazedly she began to climb down. "Spiller . . ." she breathed. And, missing a foothold, she stumbled and clung to Pod.

He supported and gently guided her down to the water. As he helped her aboard, he said, "You and Arrietty better get in under the canopy. Bit of a squeeze now because of the cargo, but it can't be helped. . . ."

Homily hesitated, gazing dumbly at Spiller, as they met face to face in the stern. She could not, at that moment, find words to thank him, nor dare she take his hand. He seemed aloof, suddenly, and very much the captain: she just stood and looked at him until, embarrassed, he frowned and looked away. "Come, Arrietty," said Homily huskily and, feeling rather humbled, they crept in under the legging.

Chapter Twenty-one

Perched on top of the cargo, which felt very nubbly, Homily and Arrietty clung together to share their last traces of warmth. As Pod let go the painter and Spiller pushed off with his butter knife, Homily let out a cry. "It's all right," Arrietty soothed her. "See, we're in the current. It was just that one last lurch."

The knife box now rode smoothly on the ripples, gracefully veering with the river's twists and turns. Beyond the canopy and framed in its arch, they could see Pod and Spiller in the stern. What were they talking about, Arrietty wondered, and wished very much she could hear.

"Pod'll catch his death," muttered Homily unhappily, "and so will we all."

As the moon gained in brilliance, the figures in the stern became silvered over. Nothing moved except Spiller's hand on the paddle as deftly, almost carelessly, he held the boat in the current. Once Pod laughed, and once they heard him exclaim, "Well, I'm danged . . ."

"We won't have any furniture or anything," said Homily after a while, "only the clothes we stand up in—say we were standing up, I mean. Four walls, that's all we'll have: just four walls!"

"And windows," said Arrietty. "And a roof," she added gently.

Homily sneezed loudly. "Say we survive," she sniffed, fumbling about for a handkerchief.

"Take mine," said Arrietty, producing a sodden ball. "Yours went away with the skirt."

Homily blew her nose and pinned up her dripping hair; then, clinging together, they were silent awhile, watching the figures in the stern. Homily, very tense, seemed to be thinking. "And your father's lost his hacksaw," she said at last.

"Here's Papa now," Arrietty remarked as a figure darkened the archway. She squeezed her mother's arm. "It will be all right. I know it will. Look, he's smiling. . . ."

Pod, climbing onto the cargo, approached them on hands and knees. "Just thought I'd tell you," he said to Homily, slightly lowering his voice, "that he's got enough stuff in the holds he says to start us off housekeeping."

"What sort of stuff?" asked Homily.

"Food mostly. And one or two tools and such to make up for the nail scissor."

"It's clothes we're short of . . ."

"Plenty of stuff for clothes, Spiller says, down at Little Fordham. Any amount of it, dropped gloves, handker-

chiefs, scarves, jerseys, pullovers—the lot. Never a day passes, he says, without there isn't something."

Homily was silent. "Pod," she said at last, "I never even thanked him."

"That's all right. He don't hold with thanks."

"But, Pod, we got to do something. . . ."

"I been into that," said Pod. "There's no end to the stuff we could collect up for him once we get settled like, in a place of our own. Say every night we whipped round quick after closing time. See what I mean?"

"Yes," said Homily uncertainly: she could never quite visualize Little Fordham.

"Now," said Pod, squeezing past them, "he's got a

whole lot of sheep's wool, he says, up for'ard. Better you both undress and tuck down into it. Might get a bit of sleep. We won't be there, he says, not much before dawn. . . ."

"But what about you, Pod?" asked Homily.

"That's all right," said Pod, poking about for'ard. "He's lending me a suit. Here's the sheep's wool," he said and began to pass it back.

"A suit?" echoed Homily amazed. "What kind of a suit?" Mechanically she stacked up the sheep's wool. It smelled a little oily, but there seemed to be plenty of it.

"Well," said Pod, "his summer clothes." He sounded rather self-conscious.

"So Lupy finished them?"

"Yes, he went back for them."

"Oh," exclaimed Homily, "did he tell them anything about us?"

"Not a word. You know Spiller. They did the telling. Very upset Lupy was, he says. Went on about you being the best friend she ever had. More like a sister to her, she says. Seems she's gone into mourning."

"Mourning! Whatever for?"

"For us, I reckon," said Pod. He smiled wanly and began to unbutton his waistcoat.

Homily was silent a moment. Then she, too, smiled—a little puffed up, it seemed, by the thought of Lupy in black. "Fancy!" she said at last and, suddenly cheerful, began to unbutton her blouse.

Arrietty, already undressed, had rolled herself into the sheep's wool. "When did Spiller first spot us?" she asked sleepily.

"Saw us in the air," said Pod, "when we were on the hook."

"Goodness . . ." murmured Arrietty. Drowsily she seemed trying to think back. "And that's why we didn't see him."

"And why Mild Eye didn't either. Too much going on. Spiller took his chance like a flash: slid on quick, close as he could get, and drove in under those brambles."

"Wonder he didn't call out to us," said Homily.

"He did," exclaimed Pod, "but he wasn't all that close. And what with the noise of the river . . ."

"Hush—" whispered Homily. "She's dropping off . . ."

"Yes," went on Pod, lowering his voice, "he called all right; it was just that we didn't seem to hear him. Excepting, of course, that once."

"When was that?" asked Homily. "I never heard nothing."

"That fourth throw," whispered Pod, "when the hook caught in our stick, remember? And I was down there pulling? Well, he yelled out then at the top of his lungs. Remember a voice calling, 'cut it'? Thought it was you at the time. . . ."

"Me?" said Homily. In the wool-filled dimness there were faint, clicking, mysterious unbuttonings. . . .

"But it was Spiller," said Pod.

"Well, I never . . ." said Homily. Her voice sounded

muffled: in her modest way she was undressing under the sheep's wool and had disappeared from view. Her head emerged at last, and one thin arm with a sodden bundle of clothes. "Anywhere we can hang these out, do you think?"

"Leave them there," said Pod as, grunting a little, he struggled with Spiller's tunic, "and Arrietty's too. I'll ask Spiller . . . dare say we'll manage. As I see it," he went on, having got the tunic down past his waist and the trousers dragged up to meet it, "in life as we live it—come this thing or that thing—there's always some way to manage. Always has been and, like as not, always will be. That's how I reckon. Maybe we could fly the clothes, like, strung out on the knitting needle . . ."

Homily watched him in silence as he gathered the garments together. "Maybe . . ." she said, after a moment.

"Lash the point, say, and fly the knob?"

"I meant," said Homily softly, "what you said before: that maybe there is always some way to manage. The trouble comes, like—or so it seems to me—in whether or not you hit on it."

"Yes, that's the trouble," said Pod.

"See what I mean?"

"Yes," said Pod. He was silent a moment, thinking this out. "Oh, well . . ." he said at last, and turned as if to go.

"Just a minute, Pod," pleaded Homily, raising herself on an elbow, "let's have a look at you. No, come a bit closer. Turn round a bit . . . that's right. I wish the light was better. . . ." Sitting up in her nest of fleece, she gave him a long look—it was a very gentle look for Homily. "Yes . . ." she decided at last, "white kind of suits you, Pod."

In the large kitchen at Firbank Hall, Crampfurl, the gardener, pushed his chair back from the table. Picking his teeth with a whittled matchstick, he stared at the embers of the stove. "Funny . . ." he said.

Mrs. Driver, the cook, who was clearing the dishes paused in her stacking of the plates; her suspicious eyes slid sideways. "What is?"

"Something I saw . . ."

"At market?"

"No—tonight, on the way home. . . ." Crampfurl was silent a moment, staring toward the grate. "Remember that time—last March, wasn't it—when we had the floor up?"

Mrs. Driver's swarthy face seemed to darken. Tightening her lips, she clattered the plates together and, almost angrily, threw the spoons into a dish. "Well, what about it?"

"Kind of nest—you said it was. Mice dressed up, you said . . ."

"Oh, I never—"

"Well, you ask Ernie Runacre; he was there—nearly split his sides laughing. Mice dressed up, you said. Those were the very words. Saw them running, you said . . ."

"I swear I never."

Crampfurl looked thoughtful. "You've a right to deny it. But couldn't help laughing meself. I mean, there you was, perched up on that chair and—"

"That'll do." Mrs. Driver drew up a stool and sat down on it heavily. Leaning forward, elbows on knees, she stared into Crampfurl's face. "Suppose I did see them—what then? What's so funny? Squeaking and squawking and running every which way. . . ." Her voice rose. "And what's more . . . now I *will* tell you something, Crampfurl—" She paused to draw a deep breath. "They were more like *people* than mice. Why, one of 'em even—"

Crampfurl stared back at her. "Go on. Even what?"

"One of 'em even had its hair in curlers . . ."

She glared as she spoke, as though daring him to smile. But Crampfurl did not smile. He nodded slowly. He broke his matchstick in half and threw it into the fire. "And yet," he said, rising to his feet, "if there'd been anything, we'd have found it at the time. Stands to reason—with the floor up and that hole blocked under the clock." He yawned noisily, stretching his forearms. "Well, I'll be getting on. Thanks for the pie . . ."

Mrs. Driver did not stir. "For all we know," she persisted, "they may be still about. Half the rooms being closed, like."

"No, I wouldn't say that was likely; we been more on the watch-out and there'd be some kind of traces. No, I got an idea they escaped—say, there *was* something here in the first place."

"There was something here all right! But what's the good of talking . . . with that Ernie Runacre splitting his sides. And"—she glanced at him sharply—"what's changed you all of a sudden?"

"I don't say I have changed. It's just that I got thinking. Remember that scarf you was knitting—that gray one? Remember the color of the needles?"

"Needles . . . kind of coral, wasn't they? Pinkish like . . ."

"Coral?"

"Soon tell; I've got them here." She crossed to the dresser, pulled out a drawer, and took out a bundle of knitting needles tied about with wool. "These are them, these two here. More pinkish than coral. Why do you ask?"

Crampfurl took up the bundle. Curiously, he turned it about. "Had an idea they was yellow . . ."

"That's right, too—fancy you remembering! I did start with yellow, but I lost one—that day my niece came, remember, and we brought up tea to the hayfield?"

Crampfurl, turning the bundle, selected and drew out a needle; it was amber-colored and slightly translucent. He measured it thoughtfully between his fingers. "One like this, weren't it?"

"That's right. Why? You found one?"

Crampfurl shook his head. "Not exactly." He stared

at the needle, turning it about: the same thickness, that other one, and—allowing for the part that was hidden—about the same length. . . . Fragile as glass it had looked in the moonlight, with the darkened water behind. Staring, staring, he had leaned down over the bridge. . . . The paddle, doubly silvered, had flashed like a fish in the stern. As the strange craft came nearer, he had caught a glimpse of the butter knife, observed the shape of the canopy and the bargelike depth of the hull. The set of signals flying from the masthead seemed less like flags than miniature garments strung like washing in the breeze —a descending scale of trousers, pants and drawers, topped gallantly (or so it had seemed) by a fluttering red-flannel petticoat—and tiny shreds of knitted stocking whipped eel-like about the mast. Some child's toy, he had thought . . . some discarded invention, abandoned and left to drift . . . until, as the craft approached the shadow of the bridge, a face had looked up from the stern, bird's-egg pale and featureless in the moonlight, and with a mocking flick of the paddle—a fishtail flash that broke the surface to spangles—the boat had vanished beneath him.

No, he decided—as he stood there twisting the needle —he would not tell Driver of this. Nor how, from the farther parapet, he had watched the boat emerge and had followed its course downstream. How blackly visible it had looked against the glittering water, the masthead garments now in fluttering silhouette. . . . How it had dwindled in size until a tree shadow, flung like a shawl across the moonlit river, had absorbed it into darkness.

No, he wouldn't tell Driver this. Leastways, not tonight, he wouldn't.